WARNI

If you are a parent or a teach__ over eighteen, put this book down now! You won't like it. You won't understand it. You will be totally grossed out by it.

The book is full of zombie butts, zombie buttification, zombie buttbardments, zombie butt-flicking, zombie butt-forking, zombie butt-pinching, zombie butt-smacking, zombie butt-kicking, rather large crapalanches, and deadly brown holes. And, as if all this wasn't bad enough, it's also full of truly disgusting animals like mutant zombie maggots, giant mutant zombie blowflies, poopigators, butt-piranhas, and rhinocerarses. It also repeats the word *Uranus* more times than is really necessary.

If you are shocked, confused, frightened, or offended by any — or all — of these things (which, of course, you are because you are an adult), please put the book down immediately and go find something more suitable for a grown-up. Like a book on fishing, for instance. Or politics. Or why children insist on reading books about zombie butts despite the availability of much nicer, more meaningful and significantly more profound books (like *The Day My Butt Went Psycho!*, for example).

If, on the other hand, you find yourself vaguely amused, slightly curious, or even excited by any — or all — of the things that you have just been warned about, then by all means be our guest and read the book. . . . Just don't say that you weren't warned.

The Publishers

ALSO BY ANDY GRIFFITHS

THE DAY MY BUTT WENT PSYCHO!

BUTT WARS!: THE FINAL CONFLICT

JUST STUPID!

JUST WACKY!

JUST ANNOYING!

JUST JOKING!

JUST DISGUSTING!

ZOMBIE BUTTS FROM URANUS!

ANDY GRIFFITHS

Scholastic Inc.

This book is a work of fiction. Names, characters, places, and incidents are either the product of the author's imagination or are used fictitiously, and any resemblance to actual persons, living or dead, business establishments, events, or locales is entirely coincidental.

ISBN 978-1-338-54673-6

10 9 8 7 6 5 4 3 2 1   19 20 21 22 23

Printed in the U.S.A. 40
This edition first printing 2019

This book is dedicated to my grandparents, Percy and Mabel, wherever they may be. . . .

CONTENTS

Prologue

There are many theories about how the univarse began, but the truth is most of the theories are just that. Theories. All we know for certain is that in the beginning there was a butt.

from *The Origins of the Univarse* by Sir Roger Francis Rectum, Smellbourne University Press, 2002

CHAPTER ONE

Crapalanche!

Zack Freeman skied down a steep snow-covered slope on a crisp sunny winter morning, completely unaware that he was about to be engulfed by a deadly crapalanche.

Crapalanche!

The very word struck fear into the hearts of even the bravest and most experienced skiers, but not Zack Freeman.

This was not, however, because Zack Freeman was especially brave or experienced.

Far from it.

No, Zack Freeman was unafraid of crapalanches because Zack Freeman had no idea what a crapalanche was.

There was an earsplitting crack.

An advance wave of nauseating stench.

But, incredibly, Zack Freeman was completely oblivious to even these telltale warning signs.

He was too busy arguing with his butt.*

"Can't we go home?" whined his butt. "I'm cold!"

"But this is fun," said Zack.

"Fun for you, maybe," said his butt. "You're not the one who has to put up with all the bruises. You're not the one who's wet and cold and freezing."

"Stop complaining!" Zack said. "I'm wearing thermal underwear and ski pants."

"I hate them," said his butt. "They make me look fat. Take them off!"

"Don't be stupid," said Zack.

"I'm not being stupid," said Zack's butt. "You are! Skiing is stupid. This mountain is stupid. I want to go home right now!"

"Well, I don't," said Zack.

"Well, I DO," said his butt. "And I say we go. Now!"

"You can't tell me what to do," Zack said. "You're not the boss of me."

"Oh yeah?" said his butt. "Well, you're not the boss of me, either."

Zack sighed.

Despite everything he and his butt had been through, they still had a lot of arguments.

The slope was gradually becoming steeper. As Zack picked up speed, he heard his butt cry out in alarm.

"Phwoar!" said Zack. "Cut it out. I'm trying to concentrate!"

---

*For those of you who are not familiar with the troubled history of Zack and his butt, check the glossary at the end of the book under the relevant entry, i.e., "Zack's butt."

"But, Zack," said his butt. "You don't understand!"

"Ha!" said Zack. "I understand all right. I understand that every time we do something I want to do, you try to wreck it. Well, it's really selfish and it's got to —"

"Shut up, Zack!" interrupted his butt. "Crapalanche!"

"Crap a what?" said Zack.

"Crapalanche!"

"What's a crapalanche?" said Zack.

But his butt didn't reply.

It didn't need to.

The snow underneath Zack was no longer white. It had turned an ominous shade of brown.

Zack's first thought was that his butt must be more scared than he realized. He turned around to reassure it, but what he saw almost made his heart stop.

It wasn't just the snow around him that had turned brown.

All of the snow on the mountain had turned brown. And bearing down on him was the biggest, ugliest, and brownest crapalanche in the history of big, ugly, brown crapalanches.

Suddenly Zack realized he had made a mistake. A big mistake. He wasn't skiing down a mountain — he was skiing down a buttcano! And nobody, not even the bravest and most experienced skiers in the world would have been stupid enough to attempt to ski down a buttcano! Nobody, that is, except Zack Freeman.

"Faster!" his butt yelled. "Go faster!"

Zack crouched low, tucked his head down, and went as fast as he dared. And then faster still.

"Not fast enough!" shouted his butt.

3

Zack turned his head. The thunderous brown mass was gaining on them.

"Maybe we could go faster if you would give me some help," said Zack. "I did save your life, you know — you owe me!"

Zack's butt's only response was to scream.

Zack felt the scream rip a hole through his thermal underwear and padded pants. Normally he would have been annoyed, but this time he just smiled. It was exactly what he needed. The force of the scream sent him surging forward, a long way ahead of the crapalanche.

Zack heard his butt whoop with joy.

"Good work!" yelled Zack as he dug his ski poles wildly into the brown muck in order to pick up even more speed. The more distance he could put between himself and the crapalanche the better.

But just when Zack was starting to feel safe again, he saw it.

The end of the slope!

The edge of a cliff face, dropping away into a deep, dark ravine.

Nobody could survive a fall like that.

Nobody.

"Reverse thrust!" Zack yelled. "Reverse thrust!"

"I can't do that," said his butt. "It's impossible!"

"Can't you at least try?" Zack begged his butt. "We're as good as dead. We have nothing to lose."

"Okay," said his butt. "Here goes."

It tried.

And tried.

And tried.

But it was impossible.

"I CAN'T DO IT!" yelled Zack's butt, causing him to surge forward even faster.

"Oh no," said Zack as he flew over the edge of the cliff and out into thin air.

"Oops," said Zack's butt.

As Zack fell, he noticed a wave of pink objects hurtling toward him at high speed.

UFBs — unidentified flying butts!

Zack gasped. He was helpless. One of the UFBs bore up hard into his stomach. Another smashed into his face. And yet another crashed into his butt.

"Zack!" shouted his butt. "Do something!"

Zack — dazed, bruised, and winded — began jabbing and thrusting his poles into the air. The unidentified flying butts were so numerous that even without looking, he was able to collect two poles' worth of skewered butts within moments. At this formidable display of butt-skewering, the other UFBs became frightened and shot off into the distance.

"Good going, Zack!" yelled his butt. "I thought we were dead for sure!"

"We are!" said Zack who, looking down, had noticed they were about to plunge into a raging butt-piranha–infested river. "Prepare to drown!"

They plunged into the wild brown water with an almighty splash.

The butt-piranhas set upon them before they'd even surfaced for air. Zack felt them attack his feet, legs, stomach, chest, arms, neck, and head . . . and then he had an idea.

He remembered he was still holding his poles full of skewered UFBs. He drew them together in front of him and pushed himself on top of them, taking advantage of their natural buoyancy to create a makeshift raft.

Zack smiled.

Not only were the UFBs keeping him afloat, they were giving the butt-piranhas something to chew on while he worked out what to do next.

But he had to think fast.

"What now?" said his butt.

"We need to paddle to the edge of the river," said Zack.

"But it's too wide!" his butt said. "The piranhas will eat the raft before we get there!"

"Then we're doomed!" said Zack, closing his eyes and feeling an immense tiredness engulf him. He couldn't keep fighting. It was time to admit defeat. To die with at least a little dignity.

"Why don't we jump onto that log?" said his butt.

Zack opened his eyes.

He couldn't believe it.

As if by magic, there was a large brown log floating beside them.

"Good idea!" said Zack, reaching across and dragging himself onto the log, just as the butt-piranhas finished off the last of the butt-raft.

Zack stood up, riding the log like a surfboard.

But the brown river was getting wilder and faster, and there was a roaring sound in the distance that chilled Zack to his butt.

They were heading toward a giant sewagefall!

Zack tried desperately to point the log toward the bank of the river, but the log seemed to have a mind of its own.

That's when Zack realized the truth.

It did have a mind of its own. Because it wasn't a log at all — it was a poopigator! A poopigator masquerading as a log in order to trap unwary butt-fighters!

Zack cursed his own stupidity.

The oldest trick in the butt-fighter's *Bumper Book of Butts* and he'd fallen for it!

The poopigator lifted its large brown head out of the water, revealing enormous jaws full of large brown teeth, and twisted its neck around to chomp at Zack's legs. Zack jumped back. The poopigator chomped again. Zack jumped back even farther. The poopigator lunged around and chomped for a third time. Zack jumped as far back on its tail as he could.

He couldn't jump back any farther without falling off completely. He looked down into the river and saw the frenzied mass of butt-piranhas following close behind.

And even if he wasn't chomped in half by the poopigator or eaten by butt-piranhas, he would be killed for sure when they went over the sewagefall in front of them.

And it was no use asking his butt to try to thrust them into the air. The sky was full of even more UFBs than before.

The situation was not good.

In fact, it stank.

It really stank.

"If only you'd listened to me, we wouldn't have gone

skiing in the first place," said his butt. "We could have been sitting at home on a nice fluffy pink toilet seat cover."

"Well, we're not, are we," said Zack. "We're about to die! Any last words?"

"Yes," said his butt. "How could you have been SO DUMB?"

Zack shook his head.

After everything he and his butt had been through together — after facing and defeating some of the most dangerous and terrifying butts in the world, including Stenchgantor: the Great Unwiped Butt and the Great White Butt — they had been undone by a common crapalanche.

The poopigator sailed over the edge of the sewagefall.

Zack caught a glimpse of the jagged rocks below.

There was only one thing left for him to do.

Zack sighed, reached down for the fluffy pink toilet seat cover he carried on his butt-fighting utility belt, wrapped it around his head, and closed his eyes.

●● ●● ●●

"How could you have been so dumb?" yelled the Kicker, violently shaking Zack's shoulder.

Zack blinked under the harsh fluorescent light, trying to understand what was happening to him.

Apparently he wasn't about to be dashed on sharp rocks, drowned in a sewagefall, eaten by a poopigator, have the flesh stripped from his bones by butt-piranhas, attacked by UFBs, or even buried in a crapalanche.

He blinked again and looked around.

He was inside a state-of-the-art butt-fighting simulator.

Buckled, belted, and clamped into a black leather chair in front of a wraparound screen. The clamps had been fitted to prevent terrified rookies from escaping the simulator. Once a simulated butt-fighting program began, nobody was able to leave, no matter how scary — or how hairy — the simulated butts and challenges became.

Once again Zack marveled at how overwhelmingly believable the environments and situations created by the simulator were. And, how overwhelmingly terrifying. They completely sucked him in every time, which, of course, was the whole point. To give the rookie butt-fighters at Silas Sterne's Butt-fighting Academy a chance to virtually experience the threats and challenges of butt-fighting before they actually had to do it for real.

But the fact that Zack wasn't really about to be dashed on sharp rocks, drowned in a sewagefall, have the flesh stripped from his bones by butt-piranhas, attacked by UFBs, or buried in a crapalanche was no great cause for celebration.

Zack was in for something that would make any one of these possible fates infinitely preferable: another tongue-lashing from the Kicker.

This wasn't the first simulated butt-fighting episode that Zack had failed. In the three weeks he'd been at the Academy studying for his elementary butt-fighter's certificate, Zack had died in almost every way it was possible for a butt-fighter to die. He'd been crushed in buttquakes, asphyxiated by stink-tornadoes, thrown off the backs of giant bucking blowflies, squashed by the Abuminable Brownman, run over by stampeding rhinocerarses, and, most humiliating of all, gassed by a simulated replica of his own butt.

Because the shiny silver surfaces of the butt-fighting simulator acted like an echo chamber, Zack could barely understand a word the Kicker was yelling as he unlocked the clamps that held Zack in the seat. He did, however, have no trouble picking out key words and phrases such as "HOPELESS!," "CALL YOURSELF A BUTT-FIGHTER?!," AND "GET OUT, I WANT TO TALK TO YOU!"

Zack took off his helmet.

"This is all your fault," he whispered to his butt.

"Me?" it said. "What did I do?"

"If you hadn't done a forward thrust instead of a reverse thrust, we wouldn't have gone over the cliff in the first place!"

"True," said his butt. "We would have been buried in the crapalanche instead! That was a much better plan, Zack. Sorry. My mistake!"

Zack climbed out of the simulator and stepped into the classroom.

The Kicker followed. He stood and faced Zack, his hands on his hips.

"What did you think you were doing?" he roared, not waiting for a reply. "Why have you ignored everything I've tried to teach you? We've been over the difference between a mountain and a buttcano a hundred times! One is filled with rock and the other is filled with —"

"Yes," said Zack, cutting in. "I know, but . . ."

"No butts!" yelled the Kicker. "You can learn to fight butts or you can make excuses but you can't do both! What's it going to be, boy?"

"I'm not making excuses," said Zack, who was getting flustered. "I'm trying to explain . . ."

The Kicker stepped closely toward Zack and bent down so his face was only a few inches from Zack's. Zack shuddered. The Kicker was frightening enough at the best of times, but up close, he was terrifying.

"Listen, boy," said the Kicker, "I'm not here to listen to excuses OR explanations. I'm here to teach you how to fight butts. Understand?"

Zack bit his lip and nodded.

"It was my fault," said Zack's butt.

"Shut up!" said the Kicker. "I sure didn't give up my summer vacation to argue with a butt. If it was up to me, you wouldn't even be here. I ought to kick you from here to the Moon!"

"Are you going to let him talk to me like that, Zack?" asked Zack's butt.

Zack trembled.

"Well?" said his butt.

"Don't talk to my butt like that," Zack said in a barely audible whisper.

The Kicker pushed his head even closer to Zack's. So close that their noses were practically touching.

"Don't tell me what I can and can't do," said the Kicker. "Don't forget who you are. When you've kicked as many butts as I have, then maybe I'll listen to you, but for now you're not even a butt-kicker's bootstrap. And the way you're going, you'll never amount to much more. Oh, sure, you might think that because you fired a harpoon into the Great White Butt and you've been nominated for the Butt Hunters' Hall of Fame that you know it all, but your performance in the simulator suggests to me that you don't know anything! You've been gassed, pummeled, putrefied, ambushed, and sat on more times than I have ever seen any trainee butt-fighter gassed, pummeled, putrefied, ambushed, and sat on in my entire life. Butt-fighting is no joking matter. You'd better get serious!"

"I AM serious!" replied Zack, surprised at the loudness of his voice. "If you'd maybe encourage me once in a while instead of picking on me all the time . . ."

"Oh!" said the Kicker. "So it's *my* fault!"

"I'm not saying that," said Zack.

"Then what are you saying?" asked the Kicker.

Before Zack could respond, the door opened to reveal the Smacker and Silas Sterne. Their enormous bodies seemed to fill the classroom.

Great, thought Zack. Just great. The only thing worse than being yelled at by the Kicker was being yelled at by the Kicker in front of other people. And not just other people, but two of the bravest and best butt-fighting warriors in the world.

"What's all the shouting about?" said the Smacker, placing her large hands on her hips. "We could hear you from the other hill. And I've got a terrible headache."

The Kicker rolled his eyes. "I'm just trying to explain to Zack the difference between a buttcano and a mountain."

"Oh, that's easy," said the Smacker. "One is filled with rock and the other is filled with —"

"I think we're all well aware of what buttcanos are filled with," said Silas Sterne, "especially Zack!"

"Yes," said Zack. "I just didn't realize that a buttcano could look so much like a mountain."

"Well, it's about time you did," said the Kicker.

"Take it easy, Kicker," said the Smacker. "Don't forget, you were a beginner once, too."

"Sure I was," the Kicker replied. "And so was Zack, but he's been here for three whole weeks now, and he's failed the simulator every single time he's been in it."

Zack looked at the floor.

Silas frowned, stroked his chin, and studied Zack intently. "I can't understand it," he said. "You showed such potential out in the field. The simulator should be a walk in the park for you."

The Kicker snorted.

Zack shrugged. He was sick of the Kicker. He was sick of the simulator. He was sick of the Academy. He was sick of being called dumb. He was sick of *feeling* dumb. And he was sick of butt-fighting.

He looked around the classroom. The blackboard was covered with masses of complicated pictures of butts being kicked and smacked, along with hundreds of complex mathematical equations relating to the precise force with which the kicks and smacks should be delivered, and the most effective angles to deliver them from. On the bench at the side of the classroom, there was a plastic model of a butt with cutaways showing its substructure and internal workings. The walls were covered with various charts on topics such as butt-fighting safety, responsible butt ownership, appropriate butt-fighting clothing and protective gear, butt-fighting weaponry, and butt recognition charts. There was also a class set of *The Bumper Book of Butts* — the official butt-fighter's encyclopedia — and at the front of the room, a bust of the greatest Butt Hunter who ever lived: Silas Sterne.

A few short weeks ago, Zack had been excited by all of this, but now it just filled him with an overwhelming sense of tiredness. The truth, Zack realized, was that he didn't belong here. He never had. He'd been lucky, that's all, but now it was time to go home.

The realization hit Zack with the force of a nuclear butt.

Of course! It was so obvious! Why had it taken him until now to realize it?

It was time to settle down and forget all about runaway butts and butt-fighting. Sure, butt-fighting had its share of highs, but it seemed to Zack that it was mostly lows. Being gassed, pummeled, putrefied, ambushed, and sat on wasn't exactly his idea of fun. How could I have been so dumb? he wondered, breaking into a broad grin.

The Kicker frowned.

"Something funny?" he said.

"No," replied Zack. "I'm just happy."

The Kicker was flabbergasted.

"Well, you'd better get UNhappy and get you and your butt back into the simulator. We're going to do this until you get it right."

"No," said Zack. "I don't think we'll be doing that."

"And why not?" said the Kicker, trembling with rage.

"Because I QUIT!" said Zack. He unbuckled his butt-fighter's utility belt and threw it down on the floor at the Kicker's enormous black-booted feet.

Everybody in the room stared at the belt — with its load of toilet rolls, clothespins, corks, and deodorant cans — lying limply on the ground.

"But, Zack," said the Smacker, breaking the silence, "you can't quit!"

"Nobody quits the Academy!" said the Kicker.

"I just did," Zack told them, heading for the door, trying hard not to make eye contact with Silas.

"You know what you need?" said the Kicker, stepping forward to block Zack's path. "A good kicking! That's what!"

"No, Kicker," said the Smacker, stepping forward to hold him back. "That won't change his mind."

"I just want to kick a little bit of sense into him, that's all," said the Kicker.

Zack ignored them both.

But as his fingers touched the door handle, he felt the strong grip of a hand on his shoulder. Zack turned around. The hand belonged to Silas. Zack studied the cracked skin. It was burned, scarred, and — in spite of constant hand-washing — stained brown from decades of raw hand-to-butt combat.

Silas crouched down in front of Zack.

"Zack," said Silas. "Look at me."

Zack looked up and met his gaze.

"I know it's hard, Zack," Silas continued. "But you've

got to hang in there. Without a proper understanding of the basics, you'll never be able to reach your full potential. The best you'll ever be is a butt-catcher. Sure, you'll be able to smack a few butts here and kick a few butts there — maybe you'll even wipe a few out — but butt-catchers don't live for long in this business. I know it's hard to believe, but sooner or later you'll meet the wrong butt. A butt with your name on it. Or maybe you'll make a simple mistake. To avoid that you need to know what you're doing and why you're doing it."

Zack nodded, but for the first time in his life he knew exactly what he was doing and why he was doing it. He'd been flattered by Silas Sterne's invitation to attend the Academy, and he'd given it his best shot, but the life of a butt-fighter was clearly not for him.

"Thanks," said Zack. "Thanks for everything. But the Kicker's right. I'm not a butt-fighter. I never was and I never will be. I just want to go home."

"Believe me, I know what you're feeling, Zack," said Silas, taking his hand off Zack's shoulder and standing up. He rubbed his temples and sighed. "It's not an easy life for any of us, but you can't escape your destiny."

"But that's just it!" Zack told him. "I don't have a destiny. I got lucky, that's all."

"Don't underestimate yourself, Zack," said Silas, staring into Zack's eyes. "You can go if you wish, but you'll be back."

"You're wrong," said Zack, tearing his eyes away from the Butt Hunter's stare. He turned and opened the door.

"Come back here!" yelled the Kicker from the other end of the room. "That's an order!"

Zack didn't reply.

His butt, however, did.

But not in English.

Zack's eyes began to water. He slammed the door behind him and ran down the steps.

He wasn't sure how the Kicker might react to a provocation like that, and he didn't want to be around to find out.

He heard the door open behind him.

"You should have got rid of that butt when you had the chance, boy!" yelled the Kicker.

Zack just kept running.

"Come on," he said to his butt. "We're going home."

●● ●● ●●

After a while, when he was a safe distance from the Kicker, Zack slowed down.

He was hot.

He wiped his brow and shielded his eyes against the midday sun.

The Academy was deserted. Normally at this time of day, the place would have been teeming with rookie butt-fighters — the crème de la crème of the Junior Butt-fighters' League — but it was summer and they had all gone home for vacation, leaving only the Kicker, the Smacker, Silas Sterne, and his daughter, Eleanor, on duty.

The Academy was spread across two hills and boasted a commanding view of the surrounding countryside, making it virtually impregnable against surprise butt attacks. Silas Sterne had started the Academy — which he liked to call his "ranch" — with the small fortune he'd amassed from the many butt-hunting bounties he'd collected over his long career. He lived in a two-story mansion on top of one of the hills. On the other hill, there was a small open-air chapel and cemetery where some of the finest butt-fighters in the history of butt-fighting were buried, including Silas Sterne's wife.

Zack walked on, between the two hills and past the yard where they broke in the dangerous wild butts that Silas would often bring back from his travels. Past the rodeo ring where the best and bravest of the recruits would try to ride them without getting bucked off, blasted off, or, worst of all, sat upon. Past the Smackatorium and the Kickatorium, the two enclosed gymnasiums where the finer points of smacking and kicking butts were taught. Past the Kissatorium, which, since they'd been unable to secure a replacement for the Kisser, was in the process of being demolished to make way for a bank of high-powered hand-washing units.

Zack smiled as he remembered the first and most important rule of butt-fighting: Always wash your hands afterwards. At least he'd learned something, he thought.

He walked past the laboratory where Eleanor conducted her research and created the silicone replacement butts that were standard issue for all butt-fighting trainees, except for Zack who had a special exemption to retain his own butt in recognition of the fact that they were a team. On he went, past the dining hall and finally across to the little rows of domed cabins that housed the trainees.

Just as Zack was about to walk up the steps to his cabin, he heard Eleanor calling out behind him.

He turned to see her running across the yard, his utility belt in her hands. She reached the bottom of the stairs, breathless from her run, and held the belt out toward him.

"I found your belt," she said. "It was in the bin outside the classroom."

Zack nodded, but made no attempt to take it from her. "Thanks, Eleanor," he said, "but I won't be needing it anymore."

Eleanor frowned. "What do you mean you won't be needing it?"

"It's just a kid's toy," said Zack, avoiding the question. "You said so yourself."

Eleanor looked embarrassed. "Yes, when I first saw it," she admitted. "But that was before I saw how well it worked. Even I wear one now. Look!"

Eleanor lifted her shirt slightly to reveal an identical butt-fighter's utility belt complete with wooden clothespins, a roll of toilet paper, a fluffy pink toilet seat cover, a small rolled-up net, a row of corks, a set of sewing needles, a box of matches, a tennis racket, a cake of soap, and a large gold buckle inscribed with the words BE BOLD. BE BRAVE. BE FREE.

Zack smiled. I'll soon be free all right, he thought. Free of all this butt-fighting nonsense.

Eleanor smiled back at Zack and held out Zack's belt. When he didn't take it, she frowned. "Well," she said, "do you want it or not?"

Zack shook his head. "Not," he said. "I'm going home."

"Home?" said Eleanor. "For vacation?"

"No," said Zack. "For good. I've quit."

"What did you say?" said Eleanor, looking shocked.

"I quit!" said Zack.

"Quit?" said Eleanor.

"Quit!" said Zack.

"You're joking, right?" said Eleanor.

"No," Zack said. "I'm not joking. I'm quitting."

"But you're a butt-fighter!" said Eleanor. "Butt-fighters don't quit!"

"I'm not a butt-fighter," said Zack quietly, "and I never will be."

He turned and entered his sparsely furnished cabin. There was a bed and a locker and, apart from a pair of standard-issue butt-fighter's boots, that was all. He reached up on top of his locker, pulled down his butt-fighter's backpack, and dropped it onto his bed.

"You can run, but you can't hide," Eleanor said, coming into the cabin.

"What's that supposed to mean?" said Zack, unzipping his backpack.

"You know what it means," said Eleanor. "You're a butt-fighter, Zack, whether you like it or not."

Zack shook his head. "I'm no butt-fighter," he said, "and you know it. And so does the Kicker. I get killed in the butt-fighting simulator every time!"

"Well, what did you expect?" said Eleanor, losing patience with Zack. "You think you can just waltz in here, pick up a few fancy tricks, and waltz out again? Butt-fighting is hard, Zack. You're going to make mistakes. We all did! Even the Kicker!"

"Well, you wouldn't know it, the way he carries on!" said Zack. He opened his locker and pulled out his pajamas. "He makes me feel like an idiot."

"It's just his manner," said Eleanor. "And I know he's been even more irritable than usual the last couple of weeks. But don't take it so personally."

"How else can I take it?" said Zack, shoving his pajamas into his pack. "He told me I should have gotten rid of my butt."

"Well, he's wrong," Eleanor said. "I had doubts about your butt at first, too, but you make a good team. You've got a great advantage over the rest of us."

"Not that great," said Zack. "We can't even complete a single simulated E-mission!"

"But you defeated the Great White Butt," said Eleanor. "How do you explain that?"

Zack swung his backpack onto his back and turned to Eleanor. "Luck," he said. "Just dumb luck. That's all. Anyway, if having your own butt is such an advantage, why don't you get yours back?"

"Impossible," said Eleanor sadly. "After the Great White Butt killed my mother, I vowed revenge. As soon as I was old enough I took the sacred butt-fighter's oath, cut my butt loose, and replaced it with a false one. That was years ago, Zack. I've got no idea where it is now."

There was an awkward silence as Eleanor stared at Zack.

Zack, feeling very uncomfortable, stuffed a couple of anti-butt energy bars and a bottle of water into his pack and then shut his locker door. "Well," he said, zipping up his jacket. "I guess I'll be seeing you."

Eleanor didn't respond.

Zack shrugged, stepped around her, and headed toward the door, but Eleanor spun around and blocked his exit.

"Don't go," she said. "Don't throw it all away."

"I have to go," said Zack. "It's obvious I haven't got what it takes."

"You've got exactly what it takes, Zack," said Eleanor, getting mad. "But you give up too easily! You're a quitter, Zack Freeman!"

"Well, that's a relief!" said Zack. "At least I'm good at something. I don't suppose you could give me a lift to my grandmother's house?"

Eleanor stared at him, her eyes burning. "I'll do no such thing!" she hissed.

"Fine," said Zack. "Then I'll walk!" He pushed past her and stomped down the steps of the cabin, willing himself not to look back.

"I never did like this place, to tell you the truth," said his butt as they passed through the front gates. "Good riddance, I say."

"You know," Zack said, "for once I agree with you."

CHAPTER TWO

The Big Bang

Meanwhile, many millions of miles away from Earth on the other side of the solar system, a tiny yellow spark flew through the freezing depths of space.

But it wasn't a spark.

It just looked like that from Earth.

If you'd been close enough, you would have seen it was a butt.

An enormous butt.

An enormous white butt.

An enormous white butt with most of the skin on its right cheek missing and its many deep layers of blubber on fire.

This was no ordinary butt.

This was the Great White Butt.

And it wasn't happy.

In fact, it was furious.

Furious at having had its dream of total buttination of the Earth ripped from its grasp at the last moment.

Furious at all the butts on Earth who had let it down by abandoning the buttcano just when it was about to blow and knock out every human being on the planet.

But, above all, the Great White Butt was furious at Zack Freeman, the chief architect of the predicament it now found itself in: hurtling through space — half dead, on fire, and too weak to stop itself.

"How could I have been so dumb?" it wondered aloud. "I should never have trusted those Earth butts — not only are they weak and stupid, but they have minds of their own. What I need is an army that won't question me. An army that will obey me. An army as ruthless as myself. But where in the univarse am I going to find such a force?"

The Great White Butt shrugged sadly and blinked.

Then it blinked again.

Although the light from the sun was very weak, it could see something in the distance.

A planet.

A blue planet.

For a moment the Great White Butt was confused, mistaking the planet for Earth . . . but as it drew closer it realized that it wasn't Earth at all.

It did, however, look strangely familiar.

Slowly it dawned on the Great White Butt that it had been here before.

Ahead of it was Uranus — one of the planets that we know on Earth as a "gas giant," and not without good reason. The planet Uranus consists almost entirely of gas — a large proportion of which is methane, responsible for giving the planet its distinctive blue color.

But Uranus had not always been this way.

Many millennia ago the Great White Butt had arrived on Uranus and encouraged the butts of the peaceful Uranusian population to rise up and destroy their owners. But although initially successful, the plan had later backfired. Freed from their owners, the Uranusian butts had multiplied out of control. In the process they had overwhelmed their planet with enormous clouds of gas, gradually choking all forms of life with lethal amounts of methane. Realizing that they would be the next to go, the Uranusian butts fled their dying planet — but they were doomed. As they entered the depths of space they were snap-frozen dead, their carcasses forming nine thin rings around the planet. At that point the Great White Butt — impervious to both the deadly methane and the ravages of interstellar travel — slipped silently across the solar system toward a small blue planet . . . and began the long, slow process of world buttination all over again.

But that was then.

This was now.

And as the Great White Butt got closer to Uranus, it began to smile.

It realized that not only did Uranus offer a means of halting its free fall through space, but that its rings could also provide the very army of butts it needed. With this army, it could return to Earth and finish what it had started with the buttcano.

As the Great White Butt hurtled toward Uranus, it

was well aware of the univarsal law of physics known to butts, butt-fighters, and schoolchildren throughout the univarse:

Methane + Flame = Explosion

Only in this case the Great White Butt realized it would be a slightly different, slightly bigger equation:

**WHOLE PLANET FULL OF METHANE
+ Flame
= REALLY HUGE EXPLOSION**

Just exactly how really huge this explosion would be the Great White Butt had no way of knowing, but it did know that the explosion would create an incredible stench.

A stench, no doubt, that would be smelly enough to wake the dead. . . .

●● ●● ●●

At that moment, James and Judi Freeman, one of Earth's top husband and wife butt-fighting teams, were leaning over a table in the middle of their intergalactic butt-mobile, about to dissect one of the butts they had just retrieved from the Uranusian rings.

James and Judi had been sent to Uranus by E-Mission Control on a top-secret E-mission to take a closer look at the rings surrounding Uranus. According to images sent back to Earth by the space probe *Voyager 2*, on its February 1986 flypast, the rings appeared to be made up of butts.

"Butt scalpel," said James.

Judi picked one up from the tray beside her and placed it in her husband's trembling hand.

James Freeman wiped small droplets of perspiration from his brow as he studied the butt on the table in front of him.

He'd dissected many butts in the course of his butt-fighting career, but never one as strange as this. It was a bluish-black color with a jellylike consistency. It reminded him of the large domed jellyfish that he used to find washed up on the beach when he was a kid.

"Are you sure we should be doing this?" said Judi.

"Of course I'm sure," James said.

Judi frowned. "But our orders were just to take a closer look. To retrieve a sample specimen if possible. E-Mission Control didn't say anything about dissection."

James drew in his breath and looked at his wife. "That's true," he said. "But then E-Mission Control didn't know whether it would be possible to retrieve one in the first place. Don't you realize the importance of what we have here? The magnitude of our discovery? This is the first proof of extraterrestrial butt life! It's our duty to find out more about it before we take the risk of bringing it back. It could contaminate the whole planet!"

"What about our butt-mobile?" said Judi. "What about us? What about our son?"

"Zack is not here," said James patiently.

"That's my point exactly!" said Judi. "He's back on Earth. All alone."

"He's not alone," James said. "His grandmother is looking after him."

Judi snorted. "Sometimes I wonder who's looking after who," she said. "What if something happens to us?"

"Relax," said James. "The butt is dead. It's a routine dissection. Nothing more."

Judi shook her head. "I wish Silas hadn't been called back to Earth. He'd know what to do."

"I know what he'd do," said James, impatient to begin the dissection. "Exactly the same thing that we're about to do. Let's just get it done and get back to Earth. We'll be home before you know it."

Judi shrugged. She knew it was pointless to argue with James when he got like this.

She pulled her butt-mask up over her mouth and nose. James did the same.

He tried to steady his shaking hand.

It wasn't so much fear that was making his hand shake as the awesome sense of occasion. It wasn't every day you got the chance to dissect an alien butt. In fact, it had never been done before. By anyone. Ever. He was about to make history.

James positioned the point of the scalpel at the top of the butt's crack and made an incision.

"That's one small cut for a butt . . ." he announced. "One giant cut for —"

"Just get on with it!" said Judi, impatient for the dissection to be over so they could start for home. They'd been away too much lately, and she was growing tired of it. Under the pretext of playing in the wind section of a symphony orchestra, they completed three or four secret butt-fighting E-missions each year. But she missed her little boy. He wasn't even that little anymore. He was twelve, and growing up fast. Although their work was vital to the security of the world, she was worried about him. Twelve was a difficult age. She wanted to be there for him in case his butt ran away like hers and James's had when they were the same age. She wouldn't have worried quite so much if her son had inherited a little of their butt-fighting talent, but he'd failed the entrance exam for the Junior Butt-fighters' League three times. Whatever his talents were, she figured, they obviously didn't include butt-fighting.

"That's strange," said James, frowning. "I've never seen a butt do that before."

"Do what?" said Judi, leaning forward.

"Look," said James, making another incision in the strange blue butt. "You can't see where I just cut."

James Freeman put his scalpel down, wiped his brow, and shook his head.

The flesh on the butt appeared to have repaired itself instantly.

"Let me try," said Judi, "after all, I did get a B plus for butt dissection at the Butt-fighting Academy."

James made a face. "Okay, hot shot," he said, handing her the scalpel.

Judi ran the scalpel expertly down the length of the crack and around the butt, neatly severing it in two with a quick flick of her wrist.

"Nice one," said James, nodding approvingly and prodding one of the halves with his finger. He had to resist an urge to pick it up and throw it, just like he had done with the pieces of jellyfish all those years ago on the beach.

But as Judi and James studied the two halves, their eye grew wide.

Judi grabbed James's sleeve.

"Look!" she said.

"Wow!" said James.

Right in front of their eyes, the two cheeks slid toward each other, and formed back into one butt.

"I thought you said it was dead," said Judi.

"It is!" said James, picking up the scalpel again. "But its flesh still retains the power to repair itself. Do you realize the possible applications of flesh like this for buttfighters? You could be blown apart by an atomic butt and then just put yourself back together again!"

Judi shuddered, reaching out to stop James from cutting into the butt again. "No," she said in a low voice.

James looked at her, suddenly realizing how worried she was.

"James," she said quietly, "it's not safe."

"How can it not be safe?" said James.

"I don't know," said Judi. "But it's too weird. I say we get rid of it. It's too dangerous. We don't even know if it's dead."

"Of course it's dead," said James. "There's no pulse, there's no electrical signals . . ."

"It may not be alive," said Judi, picking up the butt and carrying it over to the emergency expulsion chute, "but it's certainly not dead."

"But don't you see?" said James, moving around the

table to try to grab the butt from her. "Together, we can make history."

"Yes, but at what price?" said Judi. "We're just regular butt-fighters. This is way out of our league! Let E-Mission Control send a specialist team up here."

Judi was about to press the button on the chute when her attention was caught by a fiery object — a long way from the butt-mobile — passing through the innermost ring of Uranus and heading straight for the planet's surface.

"What in the univarse is that?" said Judi.

"Looks like a comet," said James, pressing his nose against the glass.

"A comet?" Judi said. "Out here?"

"I don't know," said James. "Whatever it is, though . . . it's on fire . . . and Uranus is full of methane!"

"So is yours," said Judi, "but I don't go on about it."

James ignored her. "Uranus is about to explode!" he shouted.

"How dare you!" said Judi, raising her hand to slap his cheek.

"I mean the planet!" said James as he grabbed her hand and pulled her to the floor of the butt-mobile.

For a moment, there was complete silence.

Then a massive explosion rocked the ship.

Had they been looking out of the porthole instead of lying down with their faces pressed to the floor, they would have seen a rare and extraordinary sight.

The explosion of a planet.

But while they might not have seen it, they certainly felt it and smelt it.

A blast of intense light, heat, and stench rocked their spacecraft.

As Judi flattened herself against the floor of the butt-mobile, her only thought was for their son, Zack, and how sad it was that she would never see him again.

She closed her eyes and waited to die.

●● ●● ●●

Judi Freeman's nostrils burned. Her lungs burned. Her face and hands and whole body burned as the floor of the butt-mobile became a super-heated hot plate.

She choked and coughed and cursed.

But she didn't die.

She lay there for a few moments, trying to regain her senses, and then realized suddenly that the butt wasn't in her hands anymore.

She stood up and looked around the butt-mobile. She turned to James, who was climbing unsteadily to his feet.

"James!" she said. "The butt! It's gone . . ."

James, however, didn't answer. He just stared at her, no expression whatsoever on his face.

Judi walked over to him and shook his shoulders. "James?" she said. "Are you all right?"

But James's only response was to grab her arm.

"Stop kidding around, James, this is serious!" said Judi, pulling her arm away from him.

But James didn't stop. He grabbed her arm again and pulled it toward his mouth. Judi frantically searched behind her for a weapon. Her hands closed on a toilet plunger. Not ideal, but it would have to do. She raised it high in the air.

"If you're kidding you'd better stop now!" she yelled. "Or I'll hit you!"

James sank his teeth into her arm.

"Sorry, darling," said Judi as she brought the plunger down hard on James's head, "but that's definitely NOT funny!"

James released her arm, toppled forward, and stumbled into the wall.

Judi gasped.

His butt was enormous. At least twice as big as normal. In a flash, she grasped what had happened. Somehow — in all the confusion of the explosion — the Uranusian butt had managed to attach itself to James and was making him behave very strangely . . . like a . . . zombie! But how? she wondered. Despite its ability to repair itself, the butt had been dead. At least, it had been dead *before* the explosion.

James, on his knees, turned and grabbed her ankle. Judi lost her balance and crashed to the floor. James pulled her toward him, saliva dripping from his lips as he raised her ankle up to his mouth.

Judi brought the plunger down on his head again.

James dropped her leg.

Judi jumped up, and while James was still facedown, planted the cup of the plunger in the middle of his oversized backside and with one foot in the middle of his back, began to push and pull the plunger with all her might.

James contorted his face, writhed in agony, and screamed.

But Judi willed herself to ignore him. She'd fought butts for too long to fall for a trick like that.

It wasn't James screaming, she told herself, it was the butt.

Then, as James's cries crescendoed, she ripped the parasitic butt from his body. It flew up into the air and splattered against the roof.

Judi slumped against the wall of the butt-mobile, exhausted. She sighed. At least it was over.

But any relief she felt was short-lived. As she watched, the pieces of butt-blubber slid silently across the floor toward one another, and within seconds had re-formed into a new butt.

A butt that appeared to be very much alive.

James was silent.

Judi kicked him.

"Wake up, James!" she said. "Please!"

Before Judi could do anything, the zombie butt flew across the cabin at her.

Judi stepped out of the way, but the butt hit the wall behind her and bounced off it.

Judi tried to whack the butt with the plunger, but it was too quick. "James!" she screamed as the zombie butt latched onto her butt. "Help me!"

James was still lying on the floor. He groaned and looked up. "Judi?" he said.

Immediately Judi felt an enormous surge of hunger. She was more hungry than she'd ever been before. She was mad with hunger. She could have eaten anything.

Even, she realized with horror as she lost consciousness, even James . . .

Judi, now completely zombie-buttified, reached out for her husband.

James grabbed her. "Hold on!" he yelled, hitting the butt-mobile hatch door release. Normally, to do such a thing while the butt-mobile was still in space would have been suicidal. He remembered well the lecture on the dangers of space that Silas Sterne had given at the Butt-fighting Academy all those years ago: "Exposed to the vacuum of space, your body fluids would quickly boil. Bubbles would form in your blood vessels and body tissues, causing them to rupture. All the gases inside your body would expand. You would become unconscious in about fifteen seconds. You would have permanent brain damage in about four minutes. That's if your skin wasn't punctured by small, high-speed particles traveling through space. Or you weren't instantly snap-frozen in temperatures as low as minus one hundred degrees, or turned into galactic fried human in temperatures as high as three hundred degrees in the full glare of the sun."

But as suicidal as such an action might have been under normal circumstances, these were definitely *not* normal circumstances. In all their training, not one of their instructors had ever mentioned zombie butts from Uranus, let alone given the students any information or clues about how to fight them.

Luckily, James was a fast learner. He gripped the handle of the hatch with one hand, and held on to Judi with the other.

A roaring sound filled the cabin as all the air in the butt-mobile was sucked out by the powerful vacuum created by the sudden depressurization.

It sucked everything that wasn't tied down out of the butt-mobile. Including Judi. She was half out of the ship. James could feel his grip slipping. And worse, he could feel his temperature rising. It was becoming extremely difficult to think. All he knew was that he had to hold on . . . had to hold on until the butt was sucked off Judi's body.

Finally, just as James was about to lose consciousness, he saw the butt fly out of a hole in the back of Judi's spacesuit and off into space. He wrenched her back into the ship and pushed the button to secure the hatch door.

As the air rushed back into the cabin, both James and Judi breathed huge sighs of relief, not to mention life-restoring doses of oxygen.

"I guess I owe you an apology," said James when he'd recovered enough to speak.

"Don't be stupid," said Judi. "You save my life."

"You saved mine first," he reminded her.

Judi shrugged. "We're a team, remember?" She stood up and pressed her face against the porthole. "Uh-oh."

James stood up slowly. "What is it?" he said.

"We're not out of the woods yet," said Judi. "Look at Uranus!"

James spun around, trying to look behind him. "I can't!" he said. "It's impossible!"

"I mean the planet!" said Judi.

"Oh," said James. "I thought you meant . . ."

"It's not blue anymore," Judi said, ignoring James's confusion, "it's brown!"

James peered through the porthole. "Extraordinary!" he said. "All the methane must have been burned up in that explosion. It was the methane crystals that gave Uranus its distinctive blue color, you know."

But Judi wasn't listening to him. She was too amazed by an even more extraordinary sight. "Look at the rings!" she said.

James gasped.

In their entire careers, which had encompassed many extraordinary sights, neither of them had ever seen anything quite so extraordinary.

The rings of Uranus were no longer comprised of masses of frozen butts.

The butts were alive!

Somehow the heat and the stench generated by the explosion had combined to thaw them out and bring them back from the dead.

As James and Judi watched, the butts began peeling away from Uranus in what appeared to be a mass migration.

"What the . . . ?" said Judi, her question trailing away as she tried, with great difficulty, to compress the magnitude of what she was seeing into an intelligible question. But "What the . . . ?" was the best she could manage. So she said it again. "What the . . . ?"

James rushed to the radar screen at the front of the butt-mobile.

"This is not good, Judi," he said. "This is definitely NOT GOOD!"

"What is it?" said Judi, tearing her eyes away from the awesome sight in front of her.

James gulped. "The zombie butts, or whatever they are, appear to be heading in the direction of Earth!"

James and Judi looked at each other.

"What the . . . ?" said Judi once more, although by now the answer was becoming clear, even if the question wasn't.

They both knew what had happened in the buttmobile.

Whatever the zombie butts were going to Earth for, it probably wasn't to say a friendly hello. The zombie butt they'd confronted was dangerous beyond belief.

And they'd only had to fight one!

How would the people on Earth be able to defend themselves against so many?

James shook himself to action. "We have to send a warning!" he said, urgently pumping the button on top of the radio with his thumb. "I don't believe it — there's no signal!"

"The antenna must have been damaged by the explosion," said Judi.

James thumped the control panel in frustration. "Damn these antiquated machines!" he said. "Imagine putting an antenna on the roof! That's just asking for trouble!"

"Can we fix it?" said Judi.

"Yes we can," James said, "but not with all those zombie butts out there. We wouldn't stand a chance."

"Why don't we try to race the butts back to Earth?" said Judi.

James shook his head. "They're traveling too fast," he said. "This old jalopy will only do half their speed, if we're lucky. I knew we should have insisted on a newer model. I knew it!"

James peered out of the windshield, his arms outstretched in front of him on the control panel, studying Uranus — or at least, what was left of it. Devoid of its distinctive blue atmosphere, it now looked brown and shriveled, like a piece of fruit that had been left out in the sun.

"Look," said James. "Smoke!"

Judi followed his gaze and saw a thin trail of smoke coming from a point on the planet's surface. "What do you think is causing it?" she said.

"Can't be sure," said James. "But it's probably coming from whatever it was that just crashed into the planet."

"So what do we do now?" said Judi.

James scratched his head. "I think the best thing we can do," he said, "is to go down to Uranus and try to find out what caused the explosion. It may help us to understand why and how the butts reanimated and maybe, just maybe, how to shut them down again."

"What good is that going to do?" said Judi. "We don't have a radio to tell anyone anyway."

"We'll be able to repair the radio when we land," said James.

Judi shook her head. "I don't like it, James," she said. "It's too dangerous. Besides, it's totally outside of our E-mission orders."

James put his hands on her shoulders. "In case you hadn't noticed," he said, "our old E-mission orders don't apply anymore. We've got a new E-mission now. Trouble is, we have to make it up as we go along."

"I still think we should just go home," said Judi.

"If those butts make it to Earth, we may not have a home to go back to," said James. "We have to do this. It's our only chance. If we can understand what started it, we might be able to understand how to finish it."

Judi reluctantly nodded. She was desperate to get home, but she could see the sense in her husband's argument.

They strapped themselves into their seats.

"I've always wanted to see Uranus," said James.

"James!" said Judi.

"I meant the planet!" said James quickly. "Prepare for descent."

CHAPTER THREE

The Blind Butt-Feeler

"Are we there yet?" whined Zack's butt.

"No," said Zack, shielding his eyes against the late afternoon sun. "Not too far to go though."

"You said that two hours ago," said Zack's butt.

"Well, I guess it's a bit longer to Mabeltown than I thought," said Zack.

Zack took a short drink from his water bottle, which was almost empty.

"I want some, too," said his butt. "I'm thirsty."

"There isn't much left," said Zack. "Can't you wait?"

"But I'm THIRSTY!" said his butt.

"Okay! Okay!" said Zack, squirting the last of the water into the hole he'd cut in the back of his pants so that his butt could see out. "There! Are you happy now?"

"What are you trying to do?" spluttered his butt. "Drown me?"

"Sorry," said Zack. "I didn't think there was enough left in the bottle for that to happen."

"You should be more careful," said his butt.

Zack sighed heavily and continued down the dusty dirt road.

He wished he hadn't left the Academy in such a hurry. He wished he'd thought to pack a little more food and water. They'd been walking for hours, and all he'd had to eat was a couple of stale anti-butt energy bars. He was starving.

"Zack," said his butt.

"Yes?" he said.

"Are we there yet?"

"No," said Zack.

"How much farther?" said his butt.

"Not far," lied Zack.

Zack wasn't about to admit it to his butt, but he had no idea how far away Mabeltown was, and there was nobody around to ask. Just a bunch of dumb cows that stared at him as he passed.

"What are you looking at?" said his butt.

"Moo," replied one of the cows.

Zack's butt replied with a precisely aimed jet of gas. The hapless cow keeled over and hit the ground with a thud.

"Hey!" said Zack. "Was that really necessary?"

"No," said his butt. "But it was fun."

Zack remembered how his butt had gassed Mittens, his grandmother's cat. He wished his butt could control itself. Or, at least that he could control his butt. Either would have been fine by Zack. Butts could be such a pain. And nobody knew that better than Zack Freeman. Except maybe Mittens. And, of course, the freshly gassed cow.

Zack kept walking.

He was looking forward to seeing his grandmother again. He'd been away for a few weeks now and he missed her. He was also looking forward to a nice soft bed and one of Gran's home-cooked meals.

That's when he noticed the smoke.

And the unmistakable smell of a barbecue.

It was coming from around a bend in the road.

Despite how heavy his feet felt, Zack ran to the bend and saw a small grassy embankment that led down to a river where an old woman wearing dirty gray robes was sitting beside a small fire cooking a sausage on a stick.

As Zack reached the top of the embankment, the old woman looked up.

"Hail, Zack Freeman!" said the woman. "Conqueror of the Great White Butt and savior of planet Earth! Come — I've been expecting you!"

"How do you know my name?" said Zack as he scrambled down the embankment.

The old woman looked up. Zack realized, with a shock, that she had a thick white film across each of her eyes. She was blind.

"Who are you?" he said.

The woman seemed amused by Zack's confusion.

"They call me the Blind Butt-feeler," said the woman.

"Why do they call you that?" said Zack.

"Because I am blind," she said. "And because I feel

butts. By feeling a person's butt I can tell their future. For a small fee, of course."

"What a pity we're completely out of cash!" said Zack's butt. "And we really must be going. Come on, Zack. We're very late!"

"Late?" said the old woman. "For what?"

"If you're so smart, then you tell me," Zack's butt said.

"But you haven't paid," said the old woman. She smiled mysteriously and went back to cooking the sausage, turning the stick slowly in her ancient fingers.

"Let's go, Zack," pleaded his butt.

"Not so fast," said Zack.

He was intrigued. He was also captivated by the delicious smell of the sausage meat. He couldn't have dragged himself away even if he'd wanted to.

He felt around in his pants for some money.

"What are you DOING?" demanded his butt. "You're not actually going to LET that old witch touch me, are you?"

"Lighten up," said Zack, his fingers closing around a one-dollar coin. "It's just a bit of fun!"

"For you, maybe!" said Zack's butt. "But not me! I'm getting out of here!"

Zack felt his butt begin to detach itself. He quickly grabbed it and held it out, kicking and screaming, toward the old woman.

"A wise decision, young man," she said, as she placed the sausage on a rock beside her and took Zack's butt in her wrinkled, leathery hands.

At the touch of the Blind Butt-feeler's fingers, Zack's

butt instantly became calm, and seemed to fall into a sort of trance. Holding the butt in her left hand, the Butt-feeler held out her right hand, palm up, across the fire toward Zack.

Zack stared at her.

The Butt-feeler cleared her throat.

Zack remembered the dollar and put it in the palm of her hand. She nodded, dropped the coin into her pocket and then closed her eyes, her hands on either side of his butt.

Zack crouched down beside the fire while the Butt-feeler felt. She began to speak very slowly. "Hail, Zack Freeman," she said, "glorious butt-fighter and butt hunter to be!"

Zack shook his head. He wasn't sure what he'd expected the Butt-feeler to say, but it sure wasn't that. "That can't be right," he said. "You see, I've quit the Academy and —"

"Silence!" commanded the Butt-feeler.

The fire suddenly flared up, almost engulfing Zack.

He fell backward.

"Hail, Zack Freeman, hero of free men everywhere!" said the Butt-feeler loudly. "For I can feel that you will free not just the world, but the entire univarse from the scourge of butts past, present, and future."

"Huh?" said Zack, sprawled on his back with his legs in the air. "I'm not doing any more butt-fighting in the present or the future and how could I possibly change what has *already* happened in the past?"

The Butt-feeler ignored his question. "Listen carefully,

Zack," she said. "Your future and the fate of the univarse depend on it. I have three pieces of advice for you."

Zack sat up and leaned forward.

"First," she said, "don't forget the ketchup. Do you understand? You will save the world with ketchup."

Zack frowned. "Sorry to interrupt, but I misheard. It sounded like you said 'ketchup.'"

"I did say ketchup," said the Blind Butt-feeler. "Don't forget it. And second, you must do the hokeypokey!"

"The hokeypokey?" said Zack, still trying to work out how ketchup could possibly save the world.

"YES!" said the Blind Butt-feeler. "The hokeypokey! You put your right hand in. You put your right hand out. You put your right hand in, and then you shake it all about —"

"I know how to do the hokeypokey," interrupted Zack. "In fact, it's the only dance I *do* know. But when? And why?"

"You'll know," said the Blind Butt-feeler, "you'll just know."

Zack shrugged. He couldn't make sense of any of what she was telling him.

"And one last piece of advice," said the Butt-feeler. "Fear not the brown hole!"

Now Zack was really confused.

Brown holes were the most destructive and terrifying forces in the univarse — everyone knew that. But, as far as Zack knew, they only existed out in space. And he had no intention of going there. The only place he was going was to his gran's.

But before Zack could question the Blind Butt-feeler further, the fire flared and Zack fell backward again.

"That is all for now," she said. "I am tired. And your time is up."

"And I'm getting out of here!" said Zack's butt, jumping out of the Butt-feeler's hands and taking off up the embankment.

"Come back!" yelled Zack, jumping to his feet. He turned to the Butt-feeler. "Thanks for the reading," he said, "but you're wrong. Although I did harpoon the Great White Butt and save the world, it was just a lucky shot. I'm quitting butt-fighting and going home."

The Butt-feeler smiled. She picked up the stick with the sausage on it and offered it to Zack.

Although he was starving, Zack refused. He could see the old woman was weak. He figured she needed it more than he did.

But the Butt-feeler insisted. "Take it," she said, closing Zack's hand around the stick. "I cooked it for you. You need to keep your strength up. You have a long and difficult road ahead of you."

Zack nodded, confused and yet grateful.

He turned to leave.

"Zack," said the Butt-feeler.

Zack turned around. He watched as the Butt-feeler produced, from somewhere within her robes, a red squeeze bottle of ketchup.

She offered it to Zack. "Don't forget the ketchup," she said.

Zack took the bottle, squeezed a little on the end of

the sausage and handed it back. But the Blind Butt-feeler shook her head.

"Keep the bottle," she said. "You'll need it."

Zack shrugged. "Thanks," he said, sliding the ketchup bottle into the pocket of his jacket and heading off after his butt.

●● ●● ●●

Zack ran back up the embankment.

As he ran, he took a huge bite of the sausage. It was good, but it was missing something. Of course! he thought, ketchup! He held the bottle up to his mouth and squirted some in.

He chewed the sausage.

It tasted much better.

The Butt-feeler was right, thought Zack. Well, about that much at least.

At the top of the embankment, Zack looked for his butt. He expected to find it sitting by the side of the road, sulking.

But it wasn't.

He couldn't see it anywhere.

He could, however, see his butt's tiny footprints in the dirt. He followed them up the road.

As he ran, he took another big mouthful of sausage and sucked on the ketchup bottle. His gran — a real stickler for manners — was always telling him to sit down while he ate, but this was an emergency.

He noticed his butt's footprints veer off the side of the road. They led behind a clump of blackberries.

Zack stopped.

"I know you're there," he said. "Come out!"

But there was no reply.

"Come out right now . . . or else!" said Zack firmly.

"Only if you apologize," said his butt.

Zack sighed.

He was sick of having a butt with a mind of its own. He'd had enough.

"No, actually, I've got a better idea!" said Zack. "How about YOU apologize to ME!"

"What for?" said his butt.

"For running away," Zack replied.

Zack's butt laughed loudly.

So loudly, in fact, that Zack had to pinch his nose to avoid being overcome by the fumes.

"What's so funny?" said Zack.

"I can't believe you're taking that old kook seriously," said Zack's butt. "You disappoint me. It's YOU who should be apologizing to ME for handing me over to a complete stranger without my permission."

"I don't NEED your permission," said Zack. "You're my butt. I can do what I like with you!"

"No," said his butt. "You don't own me, Zack. We're a team . . . it's the only way this can work."

Zack smiled. His butt was right. Without each other, they were nowhere. "Okay," he said. "How about we say sorry together?"

His butt emerged from behind the clump of blackberries and walked across the road to Zack.

"Sorry," they both said at the same time.

They laughed.

Zack bent over to pat his butt.

Then his butt climbed back into Zack's pants and reattached itself without any further fuss.

Zack hurried off down the road as fast as he could. He wanted to get home.

He'd been away for too long already.

CHAPTER FOUR

Zombie Buttvasion

Zack walked through the night. Although still tired, he felt much better after eating the sausage. He was also distracted by the most spectacular display of shooting stars he had ever seen. They seemed to fall all through the night — sometimes in groups of twos and threes — many with intense blue-green tails.

At first, Zack was thrilled.

He knew it was good luck to make a wish on a shooting star, and for the first few hours Zack made a wish on every single one of them. Well, three wishes actually. The same three wishes every time. That his butt would settle down, his parents would come home, and everything would return to normal.

After a while, however, Zack grew uneasy.

He wondered if it was normal for quite so many shooting stars to fall all at once. He shrugged and kept right on wishing, but when morning came and Zack could still see strange lights trailing across the sky, he realized that it was definitely *not* normal.

And whatever they were, they were definitely *not* shooting stars.

Zack swallowed hard, but his throat was dry.

And as he crested the hill that overlooked the outskirts of Mabeltown, Zack felt his throat grow even drier.

"Oh no," he said.

"What's the matter?" said his butt.

"See for yourself!" said Zack.

Zack's butt detached itself and stood beside Zack.

Below them they could see the aftermath of a massive butt-blitz. Huge cracks in the ground. Enormous craters. Most of the buildings — mainly factories and warehouses — had been badly damaged. And, if any further proof of hostile butt activity were needed, there were skidmarks all over the road.

"I thought the butt uprising was over," said Zack.

"It *was*!" said Zack's butt. "I mean, it *is*!"

"Then how do you explain all this?" Zack asked angrily, sweeping his arm across the scene of devastation in front of them.

His butt shrugged. "I've got no idea!" it said.

But Zack wasn't listening. He put his hand over his face and shook his head. "The Kicker was right," he said. "I should never have trusted you!"

"Zack!" said his butt sharply. "This has nothing to do with me or any other butt on Earth. Look!"

Zack's butt pointed to four objects — all with brilliant blue-green tails — hurtling down out of the clouds. Zack watched as the objects smashed through the roof of a warehouse. There was yelling and screaming, and then a group of four men came running out of the building with four large butts in hot pursuit.

Zack gasped.

They were not like any butts he had ever seen.

They were big.

And blue.

And very fast.

Zack willed the men to run faster. But the butts were faster still. They caught up with their prey and — joining hands — surrounded them in a menacing circle.

"What are they doing?" said Zack.

"I don't know," said Zack's butt, trembling. "But I don't think they're playing ring-around-the-rosey."

The butts advanced toward the men in an ever-tightening circle. Zack could see the men kicking and punching the butts, but to little effect.

Then, all of a sudden, the butts jumped up onto the men and squeezed themselves down the backs of their pants.

Zack shook his head in disbelief. He hadn't seen anything so disturbing since he'd witnessed the butt-catcher being rearranged at the midnight butt rally. He watched, horrified, as the men staggered around with their new super-sized rear ends, their pants bursting at the seams. It was a horrible sight. What made it even worse was that one of the men's pants had actually ripped open, clearly revealing the large blue butt clinging parasitically onto his real butt.

"I'm scared," said Zack's butt. "Let's get out of here."

"No," said Zack. "We should help them."

"No way," said his butt. "If we stay, we're the ones who'll need help."

Zack sighed. "You can be *so* selfish!" he said.

"I am NOT selfish!" shouted his butt. "I only want what's best for YOU!"

"Oh YEAH?" shouted Zack. "Since when? You are the most —"

"Um, Zack . . ." said his butt. "I hate to interrupt, but I think we're in trouble."

Zack looked down the hill.

Their bickering had attracted the attention of the men. They looked up at Zack and his butt and then began to walk slowly toward the hills, their arms outstretched in front of them.

Zack shuddered.

As the men began climbing the hill, Zack noticed their glassy eyes and blank expressions.

"That's weird," he said. "They look like . . ."

"Zombies?" said his butt.

"Right!" said Zack. "Zombies! That's exactly what they look like!"

Zack didn't know much about zombies, but he'd seen enough movies to know what they did to their victims. He went white with fear. "Get us out of here!"

"With pleasure!" said his butt. "Prepare for liftoff. Ten . . . nine . . . eight . . ."

"Hang on," said Zack. "You're not attached!"

"Oops," said his butt, quickly jumping down the back of Zack's pants. "Seven, six, five, four, three, two, one . . . BLAST OFF!"

They rose into the air at tremendous speed — up and away from the zombies and over the town.

Zack braced himself for landing.

It was going to hurt.

He knew that — but anything was better than where they'd just been

Or so he thought.

●● ●● ●●

Zack hit the ground butt-first. "Ouch," he said.

"Double-ouch," said his butt.

"That was your best ever," said Zack. "How did you do that?"

"I'm not completely sure," said his butt, "but I think it had something to do with that sausage."

Zack stood up, looked around, and tried to figure out where he was. He was in a street — that much was obvious — but although Zack knew the neighborhood well, it was impossible to tell exactly *which* street he was on.

It had the same signs of aerial buttbardment as the area where they had just been. Most of the houses were wrecked — those still standing looked like they wouldn't be standing for long. A few hardy plants and trees remained, but they had been stripped of their leaves and the ends of their branches were chewed. Skidmarks, again, were everywhere.

Zack shook his head and moved cautiously down the road, taking care not to fall into any of the freshly formed cracks. Then he noticed a thin strip of white leather on the ground in front of him.

It looked strangely familiar.

He crouched down to study it.

It was a collar.

A cat's collar — splattered with crimson spots.

With a shock Zack realized that it belonged to Mittens, his gran's cat.

Poor Mittens, thought Zack, wiping a tear from his eye.

"What's the matter, Zack?" asked his butt. "Why are you crying?"

"It's Mittens," said Zack. "They got her."

"Never did like that cat," said Zack's butt.

"That's not very nice," said Zack, shocked by his butt's callousness.

"That cat wasn't very nice to me," said Zack's butt. "Sometimes she would just walk up to me and scratch my cheek, for no reason at all! She was a mean cat, Zack."

"Maybe," said Zack. "But does that mean she deserved to die? Like this?"

Zack's butt thought for a long time. "Yes," it finally said and then quickly changed the subject. "Hey, isn't that your gran's mailbox?"

Zack, who had been too preoccupied with Mittens's collar to notice where they were, looked up at the red mailbox with the number 12 on the front. He gasped.

With a dawning horror, Zack realized where he was.

He was on Gran's street.

Standing outside her house — or at least what remained of it.

Zack stared at the house, blinking back tears.

He wished he'd returned sooner.

The mailbox was leaning so far over that it almost touched the ground. The picket fence was smashed to pieces. And there was a crater where the garden had been. But at least, Zack noted, the house was still standing, unlike the houses on either side, which were little more than piles of rubble.

Zack remembered how Gran, in one of her rare moments of lucidity, had told him that she and her husband, Percy, had built the house themselves out of bluestone. It had taken them two years, but their effort had clearly been worthwhile. It was more like a fortress than a house.

Then Zack noticed that the windows had been boarded up from the inside.

His heart skipped a beat and then he smiled to himself.

Gran always seemed to be imagining that some sort of war was going on. Now that there really *was* a war going on, it was possible that her madness was going to be her best protection. If anyone was going to be prepared, it was Gran.

Zack stepped over the remains of the fence and walked gingerly up the driveway in the fading light.

Suddenly a black shape leaped from the tree above Zack and wrapped itself around his face. He felt hot needles of pain in his cheeks.

He tried to yell to his butt for help, but his mouth was full of fur.

Zack grabbed his attacker with both hands and pulled as hard as he could. The pain was intense, but finally he succeeded, throwing it down onto the ground in front of him.

Zack assumed the kicking position that the Kicker had drilled into him at the Academy, but then he froze.

His attacker meowed.

"Mittens!" he said. "It's me! Zack!"

With a loud purr of recognition, Mittens leaped into Zack's arms.

She was thin, dirty, and bedraggled, but otherwise okay.

"Zack!" said his butt. "Check her butt. Make sure it's not zombie-buttified!"

At the sound — and smell — of Zack's butt's voice, Mittens hissed.

"Hiss at me and I'll gas you again!" said Zack's butt.

"You'll do no such thing!" said Zack, noting that Mittens's butt was its normal size. "Calm down, both of you. This is not the time to be fighting among ourselves!"

Mittens snuggled into Zack and purred loudly. Zack's butt scowled.

Zack looked around him to check that nobody was watching and then cautiously mounted the front steps and knocked on the door.

There was no reply, but he could hear movement inside. It sounded like furniture being scraped across the floor in front of the door.

"Gran!" called Zack. "It's me!"

But there was still no reply.

Zack knocked again. "Gran! Open up! It's me — Zack!"

Zack peered through a crack in the boards that were nailed against the windows.

He pressed his face up close and saw an eyeball peering back at him.

"Gran?" he said.

"Zack?" said Gran.

"Yes!" he said. "Can I come in?"

"Show me your butt!" said Gran.

"Gran?" said Zack, a little embarrassed.

"I have to be sure that you're not one of them!" she said.

Zack understood.

He turned around and bent over.

"It looks in order," she said. "Come around to the back door. Quick!"

Zack ran around to the back of the house.

He heard scraping and then the noise of the bolts being drawn.

The door opened a tiny crack and he squeezed through.

Gran slammed the door shut.

But before she could barricade it again, there was a loud crash.

Zack jumped backward as an ax head sliced through the top half of the door and a sledgehammer smashed a hole in the bottom.

Gran grabbed Zack and pulled him out of the way, just in time to avoid being flattened by the door as it came crashing inward with an almighty thud. Two people came with it and fell onto the laundry room floor in a sprawling heap.

With a shock Zack realized they were Mr. and Mrs. Jenkins — the old couple who lived next door to Gran — and that their butts were huge.

Mr. Jenkins, glassy-eyed and drooling, grabbed Zack's ankle.

Zack searched desperately for a weapon, but all he could see was a box of soap powder. It would have to do.

Zack grabbed it and brought it down hard on Mr. Jenkins's head.

The box exploded and soap powder went everywhere.

Blinded and sputtering, Mr. Jenkins still held fast to Zack's ankle.

Gran picked up the hose attached to the laundry faucet and blasted him with water.

Suddenly everything was slippery.

Zack managed to yank his leg out of Mr. Jenkins's grasp.

"Good work, soldier!" yelled Gran, grabbing Zack by the collar and dragging him out of the laundry room, and along the hall to the foot of the staircase.

Meanwhile, Mr. and Mrs. Jenkins crashed around on the slippery floor, desperately trying to stand up.

"Come on," said Gran, bounding up the stairs.

There was another tremendous crash behind Zack. He looked back and saw that the ax head and sledgehammer that had reduced the back door to splinters were now doing the same to the front.

He turned and sprang up the stairs after Gran.

CHAPTER FIVE

The Pincher

As Zack raced up the stairs — trying his best not to squash Mittens, who had taken refuge inside his jacket — the front door splintered and crashed open.

Zack glanced behind him.

Zombie-buttified men and women with huge butts were streaming into the house.

"Gran!" yelled Zack. "They're coming!"

But Gran didn't reply.

Zack looked back up the stairs.

She was gone!

"Gran?" he called.

"Up here!" said Gran. "Grab my hand!"

Zack looked above him and saw the entrance to the attic. Gran had somehow managed to get into it and was now hanging from the small rectangular hole by her feet — like a trapeze artist — with her arm extended toward Zack. Zack gasped. He had never seen his grandmother do anything as athletic as this. But he didn't have to think twice. Mr. Jenkins was already halfway up the stairs.

Zack's hand. He slid rapidly across the floor and crashed into the wall on the other side of the room. Gran slammed the trapdoor shut and then pushed a large wooden trunk over the top.

"I'd like to see those zombies try to break through that," she said.

Zack nodded dumbly, marveling at his gran's transformation.

"Now," she said, patting the wall, "where's that switch?"

Gran flicked it on.

As amazed as Zack was at his gran's transformation, however, he was even more surprised at the transformation of the attic. There was a whirring noise and Zack watched, stunned, as the roof parted and the walls slid down to waist-height to reveal a fully transparent buttproof dome. On the wall underneath the dome was a range of panels filled with blinking lights and instruments that Zack recognized as being like those in the cockpit of Eleanor's butt-mobile. He realized with a shock that he was standing in a well-equipped — if slightly old-fashioned — butt-fighting control center.

Zack could not believe his eyes.

To imagine that this had been here under his nose —

or rather, over his head — all the time he had been living at his gran's!

He wondered what else he didn't know about his gran.

In fact, he wondered whether he really knew her at all.

What was going on?

He'd suspected her of knowing a little more about butt-fighting than she'd let on. After all, she *had* told him to remember to wash his hands after fighting butts — something only a butt-fighter could have known — but he'd had no idea that Gran was involved in butt-fighting to this extent.

He remembered Silas Sterne telling him that he had butt-fighting blood in him.

Could it be that his butt-fighting blood had come from his gran? But if that was true then that would mean that his parents — well, at least his father — must have it, too. The idea seemed so preposterous that Zack could hardly believe it.

Gran was bent over the butt-radar.

"Gran," said Zack, "we need to talk."

"No time for talk, soldier," she replied, turning around. "Right now I need you to take over here."

Gran pulled Zack in front of what looked like an antique butt-gun sitting on a tripod.

"You know what this is?" she said.

Zack shrugged. "An old-fashioned butt-gun?" he guessed.

"Don't be an idiot, boy!" snapped Gran. "It's a K-TEL

three-six-zero PT-XR fourteen thousand and two point five HRH triple turbo automatic multispeed butt-splitter/ dicer and slicer. It also juices, but hopefully we won't need that — the attachment is very difficult to clean. Anyone or anything tries to get in here then you just pull the trigger! The K-TEL three-six-zero PT-XR fourteen thousand and two point five HRH triple turbo automatic multispeed butt-splitter/dicer and slicer will do the rest."

Zack nodded dumbly.

He put his finger on the trigger, pointed the barrel through a slot in the dome, and peered out into the rap idly approaching night. That's when he saw them. A horde of dark objects — each of them with the now familiar blue-green tail. Flying straight toward the control center.

"Butts to starboard!" yelled Gran. "Fire!"

But before Zack could fire, there was a deafening crash.

Despite being butt-proof, the dome shattered, spraying Zack with shards of broken glass. A group of three butts — all bluish-black in color — fell wriggling onto the floor behind him. They were twice as big as most Earth butts and twice as smelly, filling the room with the overwhelming stench of decaying flesh.

Mittens screeched and leaped from the neck of Zack's jacket.

"Well?" said Gran to the trembling Zack. "What are you waiting for? Let them have it!"

The butts, now recovered from their violent entry, picked themselves up and walked jerkily across the room toward Zack.

Zack fired up the K-TEL three-six-zero PT-XR fourteen

thousand and two point five HRH triple turbo automatic multispeed butt-splitter/dicer and slicer. Despite its seeming antiquity, it came to life in his hands, filling the attic with an earsplitting noise.

But it had little effect on the butts. They seemed to absorb the bullets as easily as a sponge absorbs water.

"It's not working!" Zack said to Gran.

"You're right," she said, holding her hands out in front of her like crab pincers. "What we need here is some good old-fashioned butt pinching!"

Zack frowned. He shouldn't have been surprised anymore by anything that Gran did, but he was. In his collection of butt-fighter trading cards he recalled there had been a card that featured "The Pincher" — a fierce-looking woman who had hands like claws and fingernails so sharp they looked like they could be classified as lethal weapons. On the back of the card it had said that the Pincher was the founder of modern butt-fighting — the leader of the very first butt-fighting team, known as "Mabel's Angels."

Zack gulped.

His gran's name was Mabel.

Zack looked at his gran and tried to match her up in his mind with the fierce image on the front of the trading card.

Could it be? he wondered. No, it was ridiculous.

Besides, the trading card biography had said the Pincher had gone missing in action sometime in the 1940s.

Whoever she was, his gran was definitely not the Pincher.

And yet, Zack had to admit, she sure had the moves.

Gran closed in on the butts, crouched over and began a virtuoso display of pinching, her forefingers and thumbs working like shears.

In less than a minute she delivered an impressive range of eye-watering pinches: two-fingered pinches, five-fingered pinches, two-handed ten-fingered pinches. Pinches that cut. Pinches that bruised. Pinches that pulled the butts right out of shape. Pinches that, had Gran perpetrated them on any regular butts, would have caused instant death.

Whatever these butts were, however, they were not regular butts.

Just as they'd absorbed the punishment of the K-TEL three-six-zero PT-XR fourteen thousand and two point five HRH triple turbo automatic multispeed butt-splitter/dicer and slicer, so they absorbed Gran's pinches.

Gran was red in the face as she prepared to take on the butts again — but whether it was from anger or exhaustion Zack couldn't tell.

"All right," she said to the butts, "you asked for it!"

Gran scooped them up, and using her arms like a vise, she squeezed the three butts together so hard they looked like they were about to burst.

Zack cringed.

Gran curled the fingers of her right hand around and pinched one of the butts. It exploded with such force it set off a chain reaction and the other two blew apart as well.

"Good one, Gran!" shouted Zack, wiping large handfuls of zombie butt sludge off his body.

"Ah, you can't beat the old atomic pinch!" said Gran, washing her hands in a small sink. "It's messy but it gets the job done."

"But where did you learn to pinch like that, Gran? said Zack.

"Well," said Gran, "it's a long story."

"Zack!" yelled Zack's butt.

"Not now!" said Zack.

"But it's a buttmergency!" shouted Zack's butt.

"Who said that?" said Gran.

"My butt," said Zack.

"There's a butt in here?" said Gran. "Don't worry, I'll pinch it!"

"No!" said Zack's butt. "I'm on your side!"

Gran looked confused. "A butt on my side? That's ridiculous!" she said. "Hold still, Zack! I'll have it pinched in no time."

"No!" said Zack. "Aaagghhh!"

"Aaagghhhh!" screamed his butt.

"Oh, be quiet," said Gran. "Both of you! I haven't even started yet."

"No," said Zack, pointing behind her. "That's not what we're screaming about . . . look at the zombie butts!"

Gran turned and looked.

The pieces of atomic-pinched butt were slowly creeping across the floor toward one another.

Merging.

Re-forming.

Into three new butts!

Zack looked at Gran.

Gran looked at Zack.

Things were not looking good.

Gran's zombie neighbors below them were not only bashing on the trapdoor, but were attacking the floor around it with their ax. It wouldn't be long before they broke through.

And the butts that were already in the attic were apparently indestructible.

"Zack," said Zack's butt, "I hate to say it, but we're not winning here."

"I know," Zack said. "Got any better ideas?"

"Pray!" said his butt, detaching itself, dropping to its knees and placing its hands in front of itself.

Zack shook his head. He didn't know what to do exactly, but he was pretty sure praying wouldn't help them.

Suddenly, however, the room was awash with light and the sound of screaming engines.

Zack, shielding his eyes from the light, looked up.

There was a butt-mobile hovering above them, and coming through the broken dome was the end of a roll of reinforced toilet paper.

Zack was amazed.

"Don't just stare at it, you idiot!" shouted an amplified voice from above. "Grab hold and climb!"

Now, normally Zack wouldn't have entrusted his life to a roll of toilet paper — not even reinforced toilet paper — but this was *not* a normal situation.

Zack looked around for Gran, grabbed her arm, and put her on the toilet-paper ladder.

"Thanks, soldier," she said. "You show courtesy toward your elders. I like that in a butt-fighter. It's so rare nowadays."

Zack was about to explain that he wasn't a butt-fighter, but decided that, under the circumstances, it could probably wait.

Gran hoisted herself up the toilet paper, as if she'd been doing it all her life.

Zack, keeping the butts away from the toilet paper with a combination of kicks and smacks, heard a noise behind him.

He saw the ax head break through the floor.

The zombies were almost in!

Zack turned.

"Hurry, Gran!" he called.

Finally Gran made it into the butt-mobile.

Zack grabbed the toilet paper and began pulling himself up, his butt reattaching itself just in time.

He was halfway up, being battered by the howling wind and the butts, when he heard meowing.

"Oh no," he said, seeing Mittens perched on the instrument panel of the control center. "We forgot Mittens!"

"Too bad," said his butt. "Keep climbing!"

"No!" said Zack. "We have to go back!"

"Keep climbing!" said his butt. "That's an order!"

"Yeah, and this is me disobeying it!" said Zack, climbing back down the toilet paper.

Mittens was now surrounded by the butts. She was hissing and scratching, but the butts were closing in.

Fortunately, however, they were all looking at Mittens and didn't see Zack coming.

Without letting go of the toilet paper, Zack reached down and scooped the terrified Mittens back into his jacket.

At that moment, the zombies broke through the floorboards. Zack saw Mr. Jenkins push the top half of his body up through the hole. Luckily the opening was too small for Mr. Jenkins to fit his enormous butt through, although he was able to make a grab for Zack's legs.

But Zack had already started climbing back up the toilet paper, even faster than before. He was almost halfway up again when the toilet paper ripped.

Whether it was the extra force Zack used, or the extra weight of Mittens, he couldn't be sure. All he knew was that somewhere above him the perforations had ripped. Not all the way through, but enough to cause him to drop dangerously low.

Zack climbed back up again, hoping against hope that the remaining perforations would hold.

One by one the tiny sections of paper ripped.

Zack inched closer.

The paper ripped again.

Zack gasped.

Then he had an idea.

He held Mittens up as far above his head as he could.

Mittens hooked her claws into a piece of toilet paper above the tear, and, demonstrating unusual strength for a cat, began to pull Zack up with her.

Just as they were negotiating the ripped section, Zack smelled smoke. He looked down to see flames racing up toward him. Mr. Jenkins, stuck in the hole, was holding a match in his hand. He had set fire to the toilet paper!

Flames were shooting up the paper ladder.

Faster than Zack and Mittens could climb.

"Hurry!" yelled Zack's butt. "I'm burning up!"

Suddenly there was a huge explosion and a fireball shot back down the ladder and into the butt-fighting control center.

"How many times have I told you not to talk when there's naked flame around?" said Zack, smiling as he pulled himself up the last few squares of toilet tissue.

"Oops," said Zack's butt, smiling as well.

Zack felt Gran's strong hand close around his wrist and pull him into the butt-mobile.

He saw Eleanor turn around from the pilot's seat, frowning.

"Eleanor!" said Zack. "What are you doing here?"

"Following orders," said Eleanor. "Dad insisted I come and get you."

"But I'm not a butt-fighter," Zack said. "Not anymore. I quit!"

Eleanor snorted. "I'm well aware of that," she said. "This wasn't *my* idea. I'm just doing what I'm told. Hold tight . . . and no throwing up!"

The butt-mobile took off at terrifying speed.

Zack looked out the window and saw the burning room they had just escaped from growing smaller and smaller. He looked at Gran, now using her formidable pinching fingers to gently scratch Mittens's ears. He looked at his butt, wiping itself clean with a towel. And he looked at Eleanor — her face gritty and desperate.

Zack smiled.

He was back in the butt-fighting front line and — he had to admit — loving it.

●● ●● ●●

"Well, it sure has been a while since I've flown in one of these," said Gran, leaning forward into the cockpit, still stroking Mittens.

"No animals in the cockpit!" said Eleanor sharply.

"Sorry," said Gran, handing Mittens back to Zack. "Do you mind if I come up front and take a look around?"

"Sure," said Eleanor. "I don't mind people. Just no cats. Too unpredictable."

"That's what I reckon," said Zack's butt. "In fact I think we should ban cats from the butt-mobile altogether."

"Quiet, you!" said Gran. "In my day, butts didn't speak until they were spoken to."

"My butt's a bit different," said Zack.

"I never met a butt I couldn't pinch into shape!" said Gran.

"You just did!" muttered Zack's butt. "Three of them."

"Hmmm . . ." said Gran, studying Zack's butt closely. "Cheeky. I don't like that in a butt."

Eventually she turned away and pulled herself through the entrance into the cockpit. "Mabel Freeman," she said, extending her hand toward Eleanor. "Also known as the Pincher."

Zack's jaw dropped. So did Eleanor's.

Zack noticed her hand was trembling as she shook Gran's hand and stuttered her name in reply.

"It's a great honor to meet you," said Eleanor. "My father has told me a lot about you."

"Oh?" said Gran. "And who's your father, soldier?"

"Silas Sterne," said Eleanor.

"Ah! Silas!" said Gran. "I taught the little whippersnapper everything he knows. Has he caught that Great White Butt yet?"

"You mean Zack hasn't told you?" said Eleanor.

"Told me what?" said Gran.

"We haven't exactly had a lot of time to chat," said Zack.

"Plenty of time for that later," said Gran, turning back to Eleanor. "First things first. What's the situation, soldier?"

Eleanor shrugged and glanced at Zack. "It's bad news," she said. "A few hours after Zack left the Academy I picked up the approaching invasion of butts on the butt-radar. They seem to be coming from Uranus."

"From my what?" said Zack.

"No, you idiot," said Eleanor. "URANUS!"

"You mind your language, soldier!" said Gran. "You're not too old for me to box your ears, you know."

"No, you don't understand," said Eleanor. "The butts are from Uranus!"

"Language!" said Gran crossly.

"I meant the planet," said Eleanor.

"Oh," said Gran. "My mistake."

"I've seen them," said Zack. "They're attaching themselves to people and turning them into zombies!"

"Zombie butts!" said Eleanor. "I should have known it! Zombie butts from Uranus!"

"Did you say zombie butts from Uranus?" said Zack's butt.

"Yes," said Zack. "Zombie butts from Uranus!"

"Language!" said Gran.

"I meant the planet, Gran," said Zack.

"The planet 'Gran'?" said Zack's butt. "I thought you said Uranus!"

"Language!" said Gran.

"No!" said Zack. "I didn't mean there was a planet called Gran. I meant the planet Uranus!"

"Language!" said Gran.

"We're talking about the planet!" said Eleanor, Zack, and Zack's butt in unison.

"Oh," said Gran. "My mistake again. I thought you meant . . ."

"Oh, this is pointless!" said Eleanor. "They're from outer space, okay?"

"I thought you said they were from Uranus!" said Gran.

Eleanor groaned. "They ARE from Uranus!" she said.

"Language!" said Gran.

"I MEANT THE PLANET!" shouted Eleanor.

"All right, all right," said Gran. "I may be old but I'm not deaf!"

"But how can you be so sure that that's where they're from?" said Zack.

"Because my dad has seen them before," said Eleanor. "Remember, he was away on a secret interplanetary butt-fighting E-mission sorting out some sort of trouble on . . . ?" She paused and glanced at Gran. She gave Zack a meaningful look. "On you know where," she said.

"Of course!" said Zack. "So this was the trouble!"

"Well, sort of," said Eleanor. "And sort of not."

"What do you mean, soldier?" said Gran.

Eleanor winced.

"Well, apparently the unmanned space probe *Voyager 2* sent back images showing that the rings around the planet Uranus were made up of butts," she said. "Dad went up there with two other butt-fighters to investigate. As you know, he was called back to help fight the butt revolution on Earth."

"So the other two butt-fighters are still up there?" said Zack.

Eleanor nodded. "The thing is, though," she continued, "the butts weren't alive when Silas was there. They were frozen. Completely dead. Something must have happened to make them come alive again."

"Silas told you all this?" said Zack. "I thought it was top secret."

"It was," said Eleanor. "But not anymore. As soon as a spectral analysis of their tails revealed that they were from Uranus —"

"Language!" said Gran.

"I meant the planet," said Eleanor wearily. "Anyway, as soon as I realized, I reported it to Dad. He told me everything."

"Any theories on how they reanimated?" said Gran.

"No," said Eleanor. "I haven't had time to study it. As

soon as we set up a ring of fire around the Academy to protect it from the buttvasion, Dad ordered me to come and find Zack and bring him back."

"Can all of you just shut up and get me some iced water?" said Zack's butt. "I got burned pretty bad back there and none of you seem to care."

"You mind your manners," said Gran, "or I'll give you a good pinching!"

"Lay a finger on me and you'll be sorry," said Zack's butt.

"All right, that's it," said Gran, reaching out to pinch it. Zack blocked her.

"You'll have to excuse my butt, Gran," he said, filling a bucket full of cold water.

"You should have more control over it," said Gran.

"I'm working on that," said Zack, sitting in the bucket.

Gran shook her head disapprovingly.

"How come you never told me you were a butt-fighter, Gran?" said Zack, trying to change the subject.

"Well, if it had been up to me I would have, but your parents had other ideas," said Gran. "They thought —"

"Oh no!" said Eleanor.

"What is it?" said Zack, leaning forward to see out of the windshield.

In the distance, illuminated by the powerful beams of the butt-mobile, he could see the Butt-fighting Academy. Or at least, what was left of it.

The entire area was devastated. Many of the buildings were either reduced to rubble or on fire. The sticks that had provided the ring-of-fire defense were scattered around the grounds.

"Looks like they've beaten us to it," said Zack.

"Who have?" said Gran.

"The zombie butts," said Zack. "From Uranus!"

"Language!" said Gran.

CHAPTER SIX

Buttmergency!

Eleanor landed the butt-mobile on the Academy landing strip.

From the ground, the devastation appeared to be even worse.

Illuminated by the ghastly red glow of the fires, it was clear that most of the buildings had been pounded from above and severely damaged.

"But how did the butts break through the ring of fire?" said Zack.

"I don't know," Eleanor said. "Butts are usually terrified of fire."

"That's right, we are," said Zack's butt. "If we're living, that is. But the zombie butts are dead. They can't feel pain, so maybe they're not scared of fire."

"But I saw a movie once," said Zack, "and the zombies in that movie hated fire."

"This isn't some dumb movie, Zack," said his butt. "This is real life!"

"Stop squabbling, you two," said Eleanor. "We have to find out if Dad and the B-team are all right. I'm going out to investigate. Zack, I want you and your grandmother to stay here."

"Oh no you don't, soldier," said Gran. "I'm coming with you. You're going to need an experienced butt-fighter out there."

"I *am* an experienced butt-fighter," said Eleanor.

"Fiddlesticks!" said Gran. "I've got more experience in my little finger than you have in your entire body."

"That's precisely why I need you to remain in the butt-mobile," said Eleanor. "If anything happens to me, then you can take over E-mission command."

Gran's eyes lit up as she looked into the cockpit of the butt-mobile. "Yes," she said, nodding. "I think that's probably for the best."

Eleanor climbed out of the pilot's seat and began to prepare herself. She pulled on a large pair of butt-kicking boots and selected two medium-sized buttblasters. Then she pulled down two buttcatcher belts. She slipped one around her waist and threw the other to Zack.

"I believe this is yours," she said.

Zack caught the belt and smiled. "Thanks," he said, putting it on. He took the ketchup bottle out of his jacket and hung it through a loop on the belt. Zack thought he'd better hang on to it. He still couldn't see how it could possibly help him to save the world, but the Blind Butt-feeler had been right about him not being finished with butt-fighting. So she might yet be proved right about the ketchup.

At last, Eleanor was ready. She turned to them and issued final instructions. "If I don't return in thirty minutes, I want you to take off without me," she said. "Go to the nearest butt shelter and hook up with whoever's left. But don't try to fight the zombies on your own. Understand?"

"Understood, soldier!" said Gran, saluting Eleanor.

Eleanor returned the salute and then looked at Zack. "Zack?" she said.

"Maybe I should come with you," he said.

"No way!" said Eleanor. "You stay here, keep out of trouble, and look after your grandmother."

"I thought she was supposed to be looking after me," said Zack.

"Don't argue," said Eleanor. "If you hadn't run away, then I could have been here to help defend the Academy."

"I didn't ask to be rescued," said Zack.

"And I didn't ask to rescue you," Eleanor replied, climbing out of the top of the butt-mobile. "Thirty minutes, right? And don't forget to lock the hatch behind me."

Zack nodded. He watched Eleanor move quickly across the yard and up the hill toward Silas's quarters. He turned back to his gran who had already installed herself in the cockpit.

There were so many questions Zack wanted to ask her that he could hardly decide where to begin. As it turned out, he didn't have to.

"If only your grandfather could have seen all this," said Gran, waving her hand across the control panels. "He would have been amazed."

"Grandpa was a butt-fighter as well?" said Zack. He had never known his grandfather. He died long before Zack was born.

"Oh yes," said Gran, her eyes misting up. "Percy was a great butt-fighter. One of the first, you know. They called him the Wiper. He could wipe out a butt from up to a mile away."

"Really?" said Zack. "What happened to him?"

Gran dropped her voice. "There are some butts that you should never try to wipe, Zack," she whispered. "Percy found that out the hard way. He was killed by Stenchgantor."

Zack gasped. "The Great Unwiped Butt?"

"Yes," said Gran. "You know of it? It lives in the Brown Forest."

"*Used* to live in the Brown Forest," Zack corrected her.

Gran's eyes widened. "You mean . . . it got wiped?" she said.

"Not exactly," said Zack. "I killed it with the smell of my dirty socks."

Gran stared at Zack. "You killed Stenchgantor?" she said.

"Yes," said Zack, "and the Great White Butt."

"So it's true!" said Gran, nodding her head.

"What's true?" said Zack.

"Once," said Gran, "on a deserted country road, many years ago, Percy and I met a blind butt-feeler who offered to tell my future by feeling my butt. I was wearing a fake butt, of course, but Percy — who always enjoyed a bit of a joke — made me hand it over. She hailed me as the forerunner of the greatest of all butt-fighters. I assumed she meant my son — your dad — but I never took it seriously. Your dad is a good butt-fighter, Zack, but not a great one. He's too gung-ho. But never, even in my wildest dreams, did I suspect that the butt-feeler might have been referring to you."

Zack's head was reeling. "Dad's a butt-fighter?" he said.

"Yes," said Gran. "And your mother."

"But I thought they were musicians!"

"No," said Gran. "At least not anymore. They were recruited at the conservatory when they were students. They just use the orchestra tours as a cover for secret butt-fighting E-missions. They're on one right now."

Zack felt his stomach drop. A terrible thought came to him. There were two butt-fighters on Uranus . . . on a secret E-mission.

"Where are they now?" he said, his mouth dry.

"I don't know," said Gran. "Their E-mission was top secret."

"But why didn't you tell me they were butt-fighters?" said Zack.

"I wanted to tell you, love," said Gran, touching Zack's arm, "but your parents wouldn't let me. Because of your poor showing in the Junior Butt-fighters' League they figured the butt-fighting blood had stopped with them. I said that it would probably just come through later in life, but, of course, there are no guarantees and they insisted. They thought that if you weren't a butt-fighter then it would be kinder — and safer — for you to be spared the terrible burden of responsibility that comes with butt-fighting and be left simply to live a normal life. In the end, I had to agree."

Zack shook his head, struggling to take it all in. If everything Gran was telling him was true, then it would explain many things, such as how he'd been able to defeat two of the most dangerous butts in the world with no training whatsoever. But it didn't explain why he'd failed so badly in the butt-fighting simulator.

"Gran," said Zack, "how do I know that what you're telling me now is the truth and not just another story?"

Gran smiled. "Have you ever wondered about the similarity between my name and the name of the town?"

"Sometimes," said Zack, "but I just thought it was a coincidence."

"It's more than a coincidence," she said. "The town was named in my honor."

"Really?" said Zack.

"Yes," said Gran. "After Percy died, I decided that if the world was going to stand a chance against butts then we had to get organized. I formed the world's first butt-fighting team with two of Percy's best friends: the Forker and the Flicker. Together, we pretty much invented modern-day butt-fighting."

Zack nodded. What she was telling him matched exactly with what he'd read about Mabel's Angels on the backs of his butt-fighter trading cards. It had to be true.

There was a sudden commotion in the butt-mobile. Zack heard Mittens screech and smelled his butt yell. His first thought was that the zombie butts had broken into the butt-mobile, but then he realized that it was just Mittens and his butt fighting.

They were having a standoff at the rear of the butt-mobile. Zack's butt had four deep scratch marks across its right cheek.

"What's going on?" said Zack.

"I didn't do anything!" said his butt, trying its best to look innocent.

Mittens was poised ready to attack again.

Zack's butt bent over, ready to blast Mittens.

"No!" said Zack.

But he was too late.

Zack's butt let fly and Mittens was blown hard against the hatch. So hard, in fact, that the force of her body blasted it open and she flew outside.

"Zack!" yelled his gran. "You were supposed to lock the hatch!"

"Sorry, Gran," he said, "I forgot."

"You've got to be smarter than that, Zack," said Gran, launching herself out the hatch.

"What are you doing, Gran?" called Zack. "We can't leave the butt-mobile! Remember what Eleanor said?"

"No, I forgot," said Gran.

"But it's too dangerous!" said Zack.

"That's exactly why I have to save Mittens!" said Gran. "It's no place for a cat! I can't just leave her out there!"

Zack glared at his butt as he quickly pulled on a pair of butt-fighting overalls, secured his butt-fighting belt around his waist, and grabbed a toilet brush.

"I hope you're happy!" he said to his butt as he climbed through the hatch.

"Mittens started it!" said his butt.

"I don't care who started it," said Zack as he left the butt-mobile. "But as usual I have to finish it!"

"Don't leave me here all by myself!" said his butt.

But Zack was gone.

His butt jumped up and chased after him.

● ● ●

Zack could hear Gran calling Mittens.

She was over near the classroom — or what was left of it. The windows were all smashed and there were holes in the roof, but at least it was still standing.

Zack headed over, his feet crunching on broken glass and splintered wood.

There had obviously been a battle of titanic proportions. It was inconceivable that Silas and the B-team could have lost, but then, where were they?

Zack heard another sound. It was coming from somewhere behind him. He glanced around to see his butt following him from a safe distance. "Come on," said Zack, feeling a little sorry for it. "Hop on."

His butt ran up and reattached itself.

Zack reached Gran. "Any sign of Mittens?" he asked.

"No," said Gran. "Your butt scared her pretty well."

Zack shrugged.

He heard a muffled cry.

"What is it?" said Gran.

"Listen!" said Zack.

They heard a low plaintive sound.

"It's coming from inside the classroom," said Zack.

They cautiously climbed the steps.

At the top, Zack pushed the door open with the tip of his boot.

The room was a complete shambles.

As Zack's eyes adjusted to the darkness, he was shocked to see a huge piece of the roof, surrounded by plaster and rubble lying in the middle of the room. Above it was a large hole through which the stars of the night sky were clearly visible.

Bookshelves had been overturned and copies of *The Bumper Book of Butts* were strewn everywhere. The model of the butt was now just a mass of plastic shards and splinters. Butt-fighting charts lay ripped and trampled on the floor.

Only the virtual butt-fighting simulator remained intact.

As for Mittens, she was nowhere to be seen.

Then they heard the sound again.

More clearly this time.

But it wasn't a cat.

It was a person groaning.

And it was coming from under an overturned bookshelf that was covered in roof rubble. Sticking out from the end of the bookshelf were two huge butt-kicking boots.

Zack smiled. He never thought he'd be so happy to see the Kicker.

"Who is it?" said Gran.

"It's the Kicker!" Zack said.

"Never heard of him!" said Gran.

"He's a butt-fighter," said Zack, kneeling down and starting to clear the rubble off the top of the bookshelf. "Don't worry, Kicker, we'll have you out in no time."

Gran knelt down with Zack and began to help him. Pretty soon they had the bookshelf clear.

"Okay," said Zack, grabbing one end of the shelf while Gran took the other. "One . . . two . . . three . . . lift!"

They lifted the bookshelf up.

The Kicker was lying on his back, covered in dust.

He groaned.

Zack and Gran leaned the bookshelf against the wall and, grabbing a hand each, helped the Kicker to stand up. He was in a bad way, swaying back and forth, as if any moment he was going to fall back down.

"Stand up straight, soldier!" said Gran.

The Kicker looked at her, dazed, as if she were speaking a completely different language.

Zack took the Kicker's arm and helped him to stand. This didn't seem like the Kicker that he'd come to know and fear. All the fire seemed to have been knocked out of him.

"What happened?" said Zack.

The Kicker shook his head and shrugged as he swayed.

Gran stepped forward. "Snap out of it, soldier!" she said, pinching his cheeks roughly.

Zack winced. You don't do that to the Kicker, he thought.

But Gran continued undaunted. "You give up, they win," she said. "You don't give up, there's still a chance."

The Kicker's only response was to open his mouth. A long trail of saliva fell to the floor.

Zack was shocked. Then he had a terrible thought. He looked at the Kicker's butt. It was enormous. No wonder he was having trouble standing. He'd been zombie-buttified!

Before Zack could warn Gran, however, the Kicker grabbed her hand, drew it to his mouth, and sank his teeth into the flesh in between her thumb and fore-finger.

Gran screamed.

But not for long. Zack watched as she quickly formed her finger and thumb into her trademark pincer shape and, as the Kicker opened his mouth for a second bite, she reached in and pinched his tongue so hard that blood spurted out of his mouth.

The Kicker staggered backward with surprise, lost his balance, and crashed to the floor.

As if it were happening in slow motion, Zack saw what he had to do. He jumped on top of the Kicker.

But he was too slow.

The Kicker launched a double-legged donkey kick that caught Zack in the stomach. Zack flew across the room and crashed into the blackboard.

Zack watched helplessly as the Kicker spat out a mouthful of blood, struggled to his feet, and advanced on Gran, backing her into a corner of the room.

"You wouldn't kick an old lady, would you?" said Gran.

The Kicker spat out another mouthful of blood and

continued his advance on Gran, who stood firm, her arms fully extended and pincer-hands snipping the air.

As fierce as she was, however, Zack didn't like her chances. But there was little he could do to help.

Suddenly the door of the classroom banged open. Zack looked up to see two large silhouettes filling the doorway. He breathed a huge sigh of relief. It was Silas Sterne and the Smacker.

Silas immediately launched himself into the room and grabbed the Kicker around the waist in a football tackle. They hit the ground hard. Silas quickly overpowered the Kicker and sat on top of him.

"Well, well, well," said Gran. "If it isn't Silas Sterne!"

Silas looked at her without speaking.

Gran frowned. "Well? Is that any way to greet your old teacher?" she said.

Silas dribbled as he clumsily got to his feet.

Zack's stomach sank.

Silas Sterne's butt was huge.

He hadn't tackled the Kicker in order to stop him from eating Gran. Silas had tackled the Kicker because *he* wanted to eat Gran.

Zack turned to look at the Smacker. Her butt was huge as well.

"Watch out, Gran!" yelled Zack. "They're ALL zombies!"

At the sound of his voice, Silas and the Smacker turned toward Zack. The Smacker lurched toward him. Silas began staggering toward him as well. The Kicker resumed his advance on Gran.

Then, behind them, Zack noticed another silhouette appear in the doorway.

It was Eleanor.

Zack tried to signal to her not to come in, but it was too late.

"There you all are!" she exclaimed. "I've been looking everywhere for you! I was starting to get worried."

Silas turned and began stumbling toward his daughter.

"Run, Eleanor!" yelled Zack. "He's not your dad! Not anymore!"

"What are you talking about?" said Eleanor.

"He's a zombie!" yelled Zack. "Check his butt!"

Eleanor's eyes suddenly grew wide with terror. She started to back away but it was too late. The zombie-Silas grabbed her arm.

Eleanor tried to break free, but the zombie-Silas was too powerful. He pulled her arm to his mouth, saliva dripping from his lips. But before his teeth could break Eleanor's skin, a dark shape flew across the room and wrapped itself around Silas Sterne's face.

Zack smiled.

It was Mittens!

Silas dropped Eleanor's arm and concentrated on trying to remove the cat from his face.

Eleanor thrust her butt-gun into his stomach and with a powerful shove sent him staggering backward toward the center of the room.

Zack looked across the room to see Gran pinching both of the Kicker's cheeks at the same time. The Kicker leaped backward — without realizing that he was on a collision course with Silas.

Zack acted fast.

The Smacker was standing in front of him.

He pulled the ketchup bottle out of his belt and squirted it in her face. She was so surprised that she staggered back toward the center of the room as well.

The zombie-buttified butt-fighters all collided in the middle, knocking themselves out at the same time.

"STRIKE!" yelled Zack's butt.

Zack tossed the ketchup bottle high into the air and watched it spin. He caught it, licked the ketchup from the top, and tucked it back into his belt.

"Good work, soldier," said Gran.

"I thought I told you all to stay in the butt-mobile," said Eleanor.

"Mittens got out," Zack said.

Eleanor shook her head in disbelief. "So you risked your life for a cat?" she said. "How could you be so dumb?"

"She's a good cat," said Zack. "She saved your life!"

"My life might not have needed saving if you hadn't disobeyed my orders, you idiot!" said Eleanor.

"Language!" said Gran.

"Language yourself!" replied Eleanor.

"Remember your manners, soldier!" said Gran. "You're completely out of line!"

Eleanor was about to reply when she heard Silas groan.

"Oh no," said Zack. "They're coming to. What are we going to do?"

Eleanor looked wildly around the room. "The simulator," she said. "We can lock them in until we figure out how to de-zombie-buttify them. I'll take Silas. Zack, you grab Kicker. Can you handle the Smacker, Pincher?"

"No problems," said Gran, flexing her fingers.

Zack, Gran, and Eleanor dragged the three heavy butt-fighters up the steps and clamped them into the simulator seats.

Then they locked the door.

"Better run a program in case they wake up," said Eleanor.

Zack opened the control panel and scrolled down the list of options:

BUTTCANO ADVENTURE

SEA OF BUTTS DIVE

GREAT WINDY DESERT TREK

STENCHGANTOR SAFARI

BROWN FOREST PICNIC

GREAT WHITE BUTT HUNT

Zack smiled. They all sounded deceptively pleasant. But he knew better.

He'd been killed in every single one of them.

Over and over again.

He punched BUTTCANO ADVENTURE. Despite the crap-alanche, UFBs, brown river, butt-piranhas, poopigators, and sewagefall, it offered excellent skiing and some of the most stunning simulated scenery Zack had ever virtually experienced.

The display offered a range of difficulty levels from one to ten. The control was already set at level ten.

That's odd, thought Zack. He was probably the last person to have used the simulator and he was only a rookie. Rookies never went past level three. Why would the Kicker have had it on level ten?

Zack shrugged, set the time period for UNLIMITED, and pressed the START button.

"Butt voyage," he said. "That ought to keep them out of trouble for a while."

He turned to Eleanor and Gran.

They were sitting slumped against the wall, exhausted with the effort of dragging the Kicker, the Smacker, and Silas into the simulator.

Zack was about to sit down when Mittens suddenly leaped into Zack's butt.

"Aaaggh!" yelled his butt.

"Aaaaggghhh!" yelled Zack.

Eleanor grabbed the hissing and wildly clawing Mittens by her tail, and pulled her clear of Zack's butt. It was obvious what had happened.

Mittens had been zombie-buttified as well.

Eleanor climbed the steps of the simulator and started unlocking the door.

"No!" said Gran, jumping up.

"Sorry, but I have to do this," said Eleanor. "This cat has been zombie-buttified! The simulator is the safest place for it."

Gran nodded sadly.

Eleanor threw Mittens inside and slammed the door shut.

"Good riddance to bad rubbish I say!" said Zack's butt as Zack dabbed at its bite-wound with a wad of toilet paper.

"Put a cork in it!" said Gran, wiping a tear from her eye.

"Language!" said Zack's butt.

● ● ● ● ● ●

"We'd better get back to the butt-mobile," said Eleanor. "It's too dangerous for us to stay here."

They left the classroom.

On their way back to the butt-mobile, Zack had an idea. "Back in a second," he said. Before Eleanor could object, he ran up the hill toward what remained of Silas Sterne's mansion.

Zack had found out enough about the true identity of his parents to become very worried about them. The co-incidence of their being away "on tour with the orches-tra" at almost exactly the same time that Silas Sterne had gone to Uranus seemed somehow more than a coinci-dence. But Zack needed to find out for sure.

He entered the front door of the mansion and headed toward the first door on the right.

He'd been in Silas Sterne's office only once before. That was when he'd first arrived at the Butt-fighting Academy. Silas had called him in and personally con-gratulated him on his success in defeating the Great White Butt. Zack remembered being completely awed by the experience.

All around the room, there had been pictures of the Butt Hunter — some of him in action, some of him pos-ing with other famous butt hunters — along with a range of certificates, awards, and trophy butts, which he'd had stuffed and mounted on the wall. Zack remembered being particularly impressed by a rack of butt-harpoons ranging from the ultra-modern (laser sighting, self-sharpening head) to the ultra-primitive (a sharpened stick with feathers sticky-taped to the end).

Now, however, like the classroom, Silas's office was a mess, bearing all the signs of a great struggle. The harpoons were scattered all over the floor, pictures and awards cracked, and the trophy butts torn off the wall and ripped apart to reveal their feather and horsehair stuffing.

Zack bent down and picked one of the photos out of the rubble.

He wiped the dust off the cracked glass and saw the Butt Hunter with his arm around a woman who looked exactly like his gran, except without the wrinkles. At the bottom of the frame was a small brass plate inscribed with the words *Me and the Pincher: Siberian Crater 1927*.

Zack searched through the rubble until he found a filing cabinet marked TOP SECRET E-MISSIONS: DO NOT OPEN.

Under normal circumstances, Zack would never have even considered disobeying an instruction like this, but whatever the circumstances were, they were definitely not normal.

He pulled open the heavy drawer and flicked through the files past a bewildering array of butt hot spots — BUTTSWANA, BUTTBAY, SMELLBOURNE, and THE NETHERLANDS — until he came to a file marked URANUS.

Zack pulled it out.

It didn't take him long to find the E-mission statement ("The purpose of this E-mission is to investigate the makeup of the rings of Uranus"), but it was the personnel list directly underneath it that made his eyes widen and stomach sink:

SILAS STERNE
JAMES FREEMAN
JUDI FREEMAN

"I thought so," Zack said quietly. He folded the piece of paper and put it carefully in the top pocket of his butt-fighting overalls.

He desperately wished there was some way to contact his parents and get them to come home. But Uranus was more than one and a half billion miles away. It was clearly impossible.

And yet Zack knew Silas Sterne had been recalled from Uranus a few weeks earlier to help deal with the unfolding buttcano crisis. If he'd been contacted from Earth then, there *had* to be a way to get in touch with his parents.

Zack searched the office for a clue.

But he found nothing.

He was about to give up and leave when he noticed a red button behind a small frame of glass on the wall behind the door.

He studied it closely. There was a small plaque attached. It read:

SPECIAL BUTTMERGENCY TRANSMITTER
To be used strictly for urgent recall of butt-fighters

on E-missions in case they're needed back on Earth to help deal with a buttmergency such as buttcano crisis, zombie butt invasion, or something like that.

INSTRUCTIONS:
1. BREAK GLASS
2. PRESS BUTTON

Zack knew exactly what he had to do.

He broke the glass.

He pressed the button.

A square section of the wall slid away to reveal an illuminated screen. A keyboard slid out from underneath it.

"Welcome to buttmergency recall," said a computerized voice. "Please type in the names of the operatives you wish to recall and supply a brief explanation."

Zack — who was not quite as deft with his fingers as his gran — typed as fast as his two-fingered style would let him.

TO JAMES FREEMAN AND JUDI FREEMAN, please come back immediately. Earth is being taken over by zombie butts from Uranus.

Love, ZACK FREEMAN (your son).

P.S. The Great White Butt is dead! I harpooned it and Silas Sterne nominated me for the Butt Hunters' Hall of Fame.

P.P.S. Gran told me everything.

He pressed SEND, pushed the keyboard back into the wall, and ran to rejoin the others.

⚫ ⚫ ⚫

Zack arrived back at the butt-mobile to find Eleanor fuming.

"You'd better have a good reason for just running off like that," she said. "Don't you realize how dangerous this place is now?"

"Yes," said Zack, "and I'm sorry, but I had to find out whether the butt-fighters who went to Uranus with Silas were my parents."

"And?" said Eleanor.

"They were!" Zack said. "So I sent them a message telling to return immediately."

"Well, that's just brilliant!" said Eleanor sarcastically. "We really seem to be getting on top of the situation here."

"It could be worse," said Gran.

"How on earth could things possibly be WORSE?" yelled Eleanor. "Zombie butts have come down from Uranus . . ."

"Language!" said Gran.

"I meant the planet," said Eleanor.

Gran nodded.

"Anyway," Eleanor continued, "these zombie butts are attaching themselves to people's butts — whether the butts are real or false doesn't seem to matter to them — all they care about is turning people into eating machines so that the butts can grow really big. Now, not only are zombie butts impervious to pain but — judging from what I saw when I rescued you both — they have regenerative powers that allow them to put themselves back together again after being blasted apart. This, according to my calculations, makes them pretty much indestructible. Am I correct?"

Zack and Gran nodded.

"And just to make things really bad," said Eleanor, barely pausing for breath, "we've just lost three of the most experienced and best butt-fighters in the world. So would you please explain to me how things could possibly be any worse?"

"At least I'm still here," said Gran.

"Oh, well, relax everybody!" said Eleanor, throwing her arms in the air. "The Pincher's here!"

"That sarcasm is uncalled for, soldier!" said Gran.

"My name's Eleanor!" snapped Eleanor.

Gran looked shocked. "If I'd spoken to my superiors like that in my day . . ."

"Well, it's not your day, is it?" said Eleanor. "Things have changed. We've moved on. The old ways don't work anymore."

"I wouldn't be so sure of that," said Gran, drawing her fingers up to her eye. "There's still a lot of pinch left in these fingers yet!"

"Sure," said Eleanor, "but pinching doesn't work against the zombie butts. No matter how hard you pinch a zombie butt it just re-forms."

"Gran," said Zack, desperate to stop the two butt-fighters bickering, "remember you were telling me how you formed the world's first butt-fighting team? Where are the other members now?"

Gran drew in her breath. "You mean the Forker and the Flicker?" she asked.

"Yes!" said Zack. "Why don't we contact them?"

"Good idea!" said Gran, growing excited. "We could get the old gang back together! Just like the good old days! Teach you young kids a trick or two!"

"Great!" said Zack, feeling hope for the first time in quite a while. "So where are they?"

Gran looked at him blankly. "I've got no idea," she said. "I don't even know if they're still alive, to tell you the truth. Last I heard, they were at the Butt-fighters' Retirement Home, but that was a long time ago."

"Can you take us there?" said Zack.

Gran thought. "I think so," she said.

Eleanor rolled her eyes. "I can't see how a bunch of superannuated butt-fighters past their use-by date are going to help us," she said.

"Got any better ideas?" said Zack.

Eleanor shrugged.

"Then let's go," he said.

CHAPTER SEVEN

The Smoking Butt

James Freeman could hardly contain his excitement as the butt-mobile touched down on the spongy brown surface of Uranus.

He pressed his nose against the windshield and peered out.

Ever since he was a little boy he'd dreamed of traveling to other planets.

And now it had finally happened.

Of course the planets he'd dreamed of traveling to had been quite different from this one. The planets in his dreams had been incredible places full of exotic plants, extraordinary life-forms, and awesome landscapes.

As far as James could see, however, the only incredible thing about Uranus was its overwhelming dullness. It was distinctly lacking in exotic plants and extraordinary life-forms, and the only awesome feature of the landscape was that it had no awesome features. There was nothing but brown sludge stretching from one end of the planet to the other.

Still, to James Freeman, it was better than nothing.

At least he was on another planet.

To Judi Freeman, however, it was worse than anything.

There was only one planet she wanted to be on, but it was more than one and a half billion miles away.

"Let's go and explore!" said James. He pushed himself up out of his seat and fell flat on his face on the floor.

Judi shook her head. "Are you all right?" she said. "Don't forget that on Uranus you're four times heavier than you are on Earth. You're going to have to slow down a little."

"Of course I knew that," said James, picking himself up off the floor with great difficulty. "I was just demonstrating how dangerous it was for your benefit."

Judi nodded. "Thank you, James, that's very thoughtful of you. Would you like me to give you a hand?"

James stretched out his hand. Judi grabbed it, and pulled him upright.

"So what are we waiting for?" said James, moving slowly toward the hatch. "Let's go!"

"Not so fast," said Judi. "We need to take a reading on the rectometer before we even *think* about going out there."

James sighed. He knew Judi was right.

He sat down in the pilot's seat and grabbed hold of a small lever that operated a telescopic rectometer on the outside of the butt-mobile. It measured the intensity of a given smell according to the Rectum scale. *A butt-fighter's best friend!* read the inscription along its side. James watched as the rectometer extended out of the nose of the butt-mobile.

When it was fully extended, he pressed the button on top of the lever marked READ.

Almost immediately the rectometer began flashing and emitting a piercing alarm. James hit the button marked OFF, but there was no response.

The needle on the dial in the cockpit indicating the strength of the stench was spinning wildly.

"Shut it down!" yelled Judi, her fingers in her ears. "We'll end up deaf!"

"I can't!" yelled James.

They watched helplessly as the rectometer on the outside of the ship began to melt.

Finally there was silence.

"What do you think it means?" said Judi.

"That we need a new rectometer," replied James.

"Very funny," said Judi. She learned forward and studied the broken dial. "Clearly the smell out there is pretty bad. Maybe we shouldn't go out."

"Are you kidding?" said James. "I didn't come all this way just to look out the window!"

"But there's nothing out there!" said Judi. "Nothing but sludge as far as you can see and a stench so intense it sent the rectometer into meltdown."

"We don't know that the rectometer didn't just malfunction," said James. "But we do know that there is *something* out there. Something that caused the planet to explode, and I'm going to find out what it is, whether you want to come or not."

"Okay," said Judi. "But we're wearing the two-hundred percent stench-proof suits. And nose plugs."

"I hate nose plugs," said James. "They hurt."

"Stop complaining and just put them on," said Judi, handing James two bright red plugs. "I'm going to take a perfume bomb as well, in case we need to clear the air."

James groaned. "I hate perfume bombs even more than I hate nose plugs. Last time you let one off I smelled like a girl for a week."

Judi rolled her eyes. "When are you going to grow up, James?" she said. "We're not going for a walk in the park. We're going for a walk on Uranus!"

"Ouch!" said James.

"I meant the planet," sighed Judi.

● ● ● ● ● ●

At last James and Judi were fully suited up in their extra-vehicular butt-fighting two-hundred percent stench-proof suits, looking more like nuclear power plant workers than butt-fighters.

"Can you hear me?" said James, testing the radio link between their helmets.

"Loud and clear," said Judi, handing him a couple of extra plugs. "You'd better take these. You might need them."

"Thanks," said James, taking the plugs and putting them in his top pocket.

Judi nodded and smiled. "Let's go," she said.

She pressed the hatch release and they climbed out on top of the butt-mobile.

Neither of them was prepared for quite how horrible it was.

Or how smelly.

It literally took their breath away.

In fact, the stench was so strong that even though they were wearing nose plugs and two-hundred percent stench-proof suits they could still smell it.

But to Judi, the most remarkable thing about the stench was that it wasn't just methane.

Mixed in was the faint, but distinct, smell of meat cooking.

"I know this sounds crazy," said Judi. "But can you smell a barbecue?"

James nodded. "Yes!" he said. "But how is that possible?"

"I don't know," said Judi. "There's a lot I don't know about Uranus."

"That makes two of us," said James, smirking.

"I meant the *planet*," said Judi.

"So did I," said James.

James turned around slowly, scanning the horizon until he located a thin plume of gray smoke in the distance coming from a crater.

"Look," said James pointing. "Over there."

Judi shifted her gaze to where he was pointing. "What do you think it is?"

"I don't know," said James. "But I think it's what we're looking for."

James climbed carefully down the ladder on the side of the butt-mobile.

"This is one small step for a man," he said solemnly as his foot was about to touch the planet. "One stinky step for mankind."

James jumped lightly off the bottom of the ladder.

Immediately, he sank down into soft brown sludge, almost up to his knees.

"Aaagghh!" he said, with a horrified expression on his face. "It's . . . it's . . ."

"It's quite obvious what it is," said Judi. "What were you expecting . . . chocolate?"

"I don't know," said James. "I've never been here before!"

"Didn't the name of the planet give you even a tiny clue as to what it might be made of?" said Judi.

"No," said James, frowning. "I thought it was named after the Greek god Uranus. The Ancient Greeks believed Uranus gave heat, light, and rain to the Earth. He was also the husband of Gaea and the father of the Cyclopes, the Titans, Rhea, and the monsters with one hundred heads and fifty mouths."

"Boy, have you got a lot to learn," said Judi.

James groaned.

"Come on, James!" said Judi. "Pull yourself together. It could be worse!"

"How in the univarse could I possibly be in a worse position than being up to my knees in this stuff?" he said.

Judi laughed. "You could be up to your neck in it!" she said "Or upside down!"

"Very funny," said James.

He helped Judi down into the sludge and they waded off in the direction of the smoke.

It was hard, slow going.

While they waded, Judi tried to distract herself by imagining what Zack might be doing right at that moment. She worked out that it was bedtime back on Earth. She imagined he was probably tucked up in bed reading — no doubt one of the interplanetary butt-fighting comics he loved so much. About this time, Gran would probably be bringing him a warm cup of cocoa and kissing him good night.

Judi felt an intense pang of regret. She longed to be back home. Zack was lucky to have his grandmother to look after him, sure, but there were some things that only a mother could do.

Judi bit her lip. She was resolved. Despite her love of butt-fighting, this was definitely going to be the last E-mission she went on. At least until Zack was grown up.

●● ●● ●●

The air was thick with smoke by the time they finally made it to the crater they had seen from the roof of the butt-mobile. It seemed much bigger up close. It was at least twenty yards in diameter. Whatever had created it was obviously very large and very heavy.

"Wait here," said James, taking a roll of double-strength four-ply reinforced toilet tissue and tying it around his waist.

"What are you going to do?" said Judi.

"I'm going to go as close to the edge as I can and see if I can get a look at whatever it is that's down there," said James.

"Be careful, James," said Judi. "It's very slippery."

"I know," he said, handing her the toilet roll. "Hold on to this."

Judi took the toilet roll and attached it to the lockable toilet roll holder on her suit.

Holding on to the other end, James waded as close as he dared to the edge of the crater and peered down into the smoking hole.

Despite the smoke and the darkness, he could see flames a long, long way below him.

"What can you see?" said Judi, through his earpiece.

"I'm not sure," said James. "Something's on fire — I can't see it because there's too much smoke. Although, judging by the smell, it's obviously animal in origin."

"But that's ridiculous," said Judi. "What sort of animal flies through space and crashes into planets?"

"I . . . I . . . don't know," said James, who was beginning to feel strangely dizzy. Whether it was from the extreme height or the smoke or the stench he couldn't be sure, but it took every bit of concentration and willpower that he could muster to stop himself from falling forward.

"Are you feeling all right, James?" said Judi.

"Yes," he lied. "I'm fine."

"Why don't you take some photos with the infra-brown camera?" said Judi, taking it out of her suit. "That should cut through the smoke and give us a much better look at whatever's down there."

Judi threw the camera across to James. But her throw was slightly too high.

James lunged to catch the camera as it sailed over his shoulder.

He caught it, but as he landed he failed to take into account the fact that he was four times as heavy as he was on Earth. He staggered backward.

Judi saw him disappear over the edge of the crater.

She screamed into her headset.

"Hey! Quit it!" said James. "That hurts!"

"James?" said Judi.

"I'm okay," said James. "I haven't fallen far. But I'm going to need your help to get back up."

"All right," said Judi, cautiously approaching the edge of the crater.

She reached the place where James had been standing and looked over the edge. James was about a yard below, hugging the inside wall of the crater.

"Give me your hand," he said.

Judi leaned forward as far as she could, but still couldn't quite reach James's hand.

"Great!" said James. "Just a little bit more!"

She leaned forward a little bit more . . . .

. . . and a little bit more

. . . and just a tiny little bit more

. . . and

. . . finally the tips of her fingers touched the tips of James's fingers.

She leaned forward just a little bit more . . .

and then . . .

just a little too far.

She felt herself tumbling forward, but there was nothing she could do to stop herself.

James grabbed her hand, but the weight of her falling body ripped him from his precarious grip on the side of the crater and they both tumbled headlong down into its murky depths.

James and Judi fell for a long time.

But they didn't die.

Now, normally, falling into a very deep hole on top of a burning unidentified alien life-form on a planet more than one and a half billion miles away from Earth on the far side of the solar system would mean certain death for even the boldest and bravest butt-fighters in the world.

But not James and Judi Freeman.

Falling into a very deep hole on top of a burning unidentified alien life-form on a planet more than one and a half billion miles away from Earth on the far side of the solar system was just another day at the office for them.

They were tough. They were also extremely lucky.

They landed in a warm spongy crevasse. They were wedged in pretty tightly but after much struggling they managed to pull themselves out.

"Phew," said James, lying on his back. "That was lucky!"

"That all depends on your definition of 'lucky,'" said Judi, opening her eyes and looking at the leaping flames all around them.

"Well," said James, "we're not dead, are we?"

"Not yet," said Judi.

She reached for the portable fire extinguisher she carried on her belt and began spraying.

Gradually the flames gave way to great clouds of hissing steam.

"I can't believe you brought a fire extinguisher!" said James.

"A good butt-fighter is always prepared!" said Judi.

James shook his head in admiration. "What do you think it is?" he said.

The object they were standing on seemed to be divided into two main sections by the huge crevasse they'd just crawled out of.

Judi knelt and examined the burned surface. "It's definitely animal," she said.

"Do you think it's alive?" said James.

"Only just," she said.

James rubbed his chin. He studied the crevasse and the two large mounds on either side. "You know," he said. "If I didn't know better, I'd say we were standing on top of an enormous butt."

"But that's ridiculous," said Judi. "There's only one butt in the world this big . . ."

"Yes," said James. "The Great White Butt! But this butt is definitely not white."

"Hang on a minute," said Judi. She peeled away a blackened layer of charcoal to reveal a blinding white patch of flesh underneath. It was so white it glowed, as if lit from within.

It was so bright that both James and Judi had to shield their eyes.

"It *is* the Great White Butt!" said James, shaking his head.

"But what's it doing out here?" said Judi.

"Remember that book *Chariots of the Butts* by Eric von Dunnycan?" said James. "The one where he postulated that the Great White Butt was a space traveler?"

Judi snorted. "That load of rubbish! What about it?"

"Maybe it wasn't such a load of rubbish after all," said James. "Maybe he was right. There's a lot we don't know about the Great White Butt."

They were both amazed and silent as they let the possibility that they were standing on top of the Great White Butt sink in.

Judi slammed her fist into her hand. "Of course! We should have known that the Great White Butt was behind the reanimation of the Uranusian butts!"

"Maybe, maybe not," said James, deep in thought. "Incredible as it seems, it might have been purely accidental."

"How do you mean?" said Judi.

"Well," said James, "it's had a run-in with something. Obviously something very powerful. Something that caused it to catch on fire and fly through space, and then — by total fluke, bad luck, or both — crash into a planet full of methane, and create an explosion so intense and so smelly that it brought the dead to life again. Now call me stupid if you like, but isn't that a possibility?"

"Yes, it's possible," Judi consented. "But the *real* question is, how do we finish it off?"

"I don't think we need to," said James. "There's nothing we can do to it that hasn't been done already. It may not have long to live. I say we get out of here, fill in the hole, and erect a monument."

"I agree," said Judi. "But let's skip the monument."

"Okeydoke," said James.

"Just one question," said Judi.

"What's that?" said James.

"How do we get out of a very deep hole with slippery sides with no handholds on a planet more than one and a half billion miles away from Earth on the far side of the solar system where we weigh four times our normal weight?"

"I've got no idea," said James, shrugging. "I was hoping you could tell me."

CHAPTER EIGHT

The Forker and the Flicker

Meanwhile, on the other side of the solar system, Eleanor, Zack, and Gran were speeding into a fiery red sunrise toward the Butt-fighters' Retirement Home.

"Red sky at night, butt-fighter's delight," said Gran as she peered over the top of her glasses. "Red sky in the morning . . . butt-fighter's warning."

"You don't really believe that nonsense, do you?" said Eleanor.

"Believe it?" said Gran. "I'll have you know, I made that 'nonsense' up!"

Eleanor clapped her hand to her forehead. "Of course," she said, "I should have known."

"When you've been fighting butts for as long as I have," said Gran, "you notice things. After a hard day's butt-fighting, the redness in the sky at night is caused by the refraction of the sun's rays through the huge amount of gas emitted by slaughtered butts."

"The death stink," said Zack, remembering the Great White Butt's outpouring in the buttcano.

"Yes," said Gran, "that's right. And that's good. But redness in the morning is *not* good. The gas should have cleared by then. Redness in the morning can mean only one thing. That butts have been active all night — plotting, scheming, and marshaling their forces."

Eleanor and Zack looked at each other and nodded. Now that it had been explained, it made perfect sense.

"Watch out!" said Gran. "Butt to starboard!"

Eleanor looked to her right and caught a glimpse of a zombie butt flying toward them. She tried to take evasive action, but was too late. The zombie butt splattered against the windshield, leaving a blue-black smear on the glass.

"I hate that!" said Eleanor, reaching for the windshield wipers switch. She flicked it a few times and cursed again. "And these windshield wipers stink!"

"Language!" said Gran.

"How am I supposed to fly the butt-mobile if the windshield wipers are broken?" said Eleanor.

Gran shook her head. "In the old days," she said, "we didn't have windshield wipers! We had to get out and wipe the windshield clean with our sleeves." Eleanor rolled her eyes. "If we were lucky enough to have a windshield, that is," said Gran, ignoring her. "Or sleeves for that matter. There was no protective butt-fighting gear in those days, you know, and certainly no specialized butt-fighting weapons. You were lucky if you had a sharp stick and a raincoat. But it made us inventive. We had to be resourceful. But nowadays . . . you kids don't know how easy you've got it."

"Maybe we've got better equipment," said Eleanor, through gritted teeth, "but nowadays the butts are meaner and more dangerous."

Gran stared at Eleanor, a wild look in her eyes. "Are you trying to tell me that Buttzilla wasn't mean?" she said. "And are you trying to tell me that the Abuminable Brownman wasn't dangerous? I've pinched butts that would make your nostril hairs stand on end, soldier. I've pinched butts that would make your nostril hairs take fright and run away. I've pinched butts that would make your nostril hairs commit nostril-hairicide rather than endure the stench emanating from these beasts! You ought to be thankful that I finished them off before you were born!"

"If you were so brave," said Eleanor, "then why didn't you get rid of the Great White Butt before it had a chance to kill my mother?"

"I'm sorry," said Gran putting her hand on Eleanor's shoulder. "I'm not infallible. If I could go back in time and kill that monster, I would. But we didn't realize just how powerful — or how evil — it was back then. In those days it was just one of many."

"Look out!" said Zack. Two zombie butts were flying directly toward them.

"Zack?" said Eleanor, wiping her eyes. "What's happening?"

But Zack had already grabbed the wheel.

He jerked it to the left, narrowly avoiding the first

butt, and then jerked it hard right, barely avoiding a collision with the second one.

The sudden turn, however, threw the ship around so violently that Eleanor and Gran were thrown from their seats.

"Zack!" yelled Eleanor, picking herself up. "What did you do that for?"

"Zombie butts!" said Zack. "You were too busy arguing to see."

"It was my fault," said Gran quickly. "I distracted you, Eleanor. I'm sorry."

Eleanor shrugged. "No, I'm sorry," she said, extending her hand toward Gran. "I guess butt-fighting is not — and never has been — easy."

Gran nodded, took Eleanor's hand, and shook it.

Zack smiled. It was good to see Eleanor and Gran making their peace. But the smile was quickly wiped from his face by what he saw when he turned and looked out the windshield.

The rest home for retired butt-fighters was directly in front of them.

But the scene was anything but restful.

At the front of the main building, there was a massive battle going on between two elderly butt-fighters and a swarm of zombie butts.

"That's them!" said Gran. "My old team! The Flicker and the Forker!"

"Looks like they've come out of retirement," said Zack.

Eleanor immediately cut the butt-mobile engines and began to descend.

Zack stared at the scene in front of him.

One of the butt-fighters appeared to be naked except for a green towel around his waist and a yellow towel on his head. In his hand, he was brandishing a large red beach towel like a bullwhip, his mighty flicks cracking like gunshots against the hides of the zombie butts swarming around him.

Meanwhile, the other butt-fighter — a huge man wearing a gardening apron and black rubber kneepads — was spearing zombie butts in midair with a seemingly inexhaustible combination of gardening and kitchen forks that hung from two belts strung across his chest.

"All right," said Eleanor, gliding the butt-mobile to a silent landing at the back of the retirement home. "Let's get suited up fast and get out there! They look like they could use some help."

Zack pulled down one of the butt-fighting suits. He chose a brown one to help camouflage him.

"I don't want to go out there," said Zack's butt as Zack put on the suit.

"Why not?" said Zack.

"I don't like zombie butts," it said.

"Me, neither," said Zack. "But that's exactly why we have to go. If we don't fight them, everybody in the entire world will end up zombie-buttified — including you and me — and we'll like that even less."

Zack checked his belt to make sure his ketchup bottle was still attached.

Eleanor opened the hatch and they all climbed out.

The grounds, apart from zombie butt blast craters, were beautifully kept. The butt-fighters ran crouching across a carefully manicured croquet lawn, past a sauna room located at the rear of the main building, and then cautiously made their way around the side. As they drew closer to the action, the sounds of the fighting grew louder and more frightening. Zack could hear the gunshotlike cracks of the Flicker's whip and the sickening squelches each time the Forker's fork connected with a zombie butt.

Eleanor nodded, signaling for Zack to go first. He edged up to the front of the building, closely followed by Gran.

The Forker and the Flicker had their backs turned to them. Their attention was completely focused on a large blue butt cannonballing toward them at high speed.

"Should we let them know we're here?" said Zack.

"What, and spoil the surprise?" said Gran. "Not on your life. Watch this!"

Gran ran up behind the Forker and the Flicker and — with a mighty leap up onto both of their shoulders — grabbed the incoming butt and pinched it so hard that it burst apart like a rotten watermelon. Well, like a burst-apart rotten watermelon except *much* smellier. *And* able to slowly reassemble itself — an ability for which it must be said that burst-apart rotten watermelons are not generally well noted.

Gran fell back down into the middle of the pieces that were already beginning to move toward one another.

The Forker turned around, grabbed a large fork from his belt, and plunged it down toward Gran.

Zack gasped.

But he needn't have worried.

Gran rolled quickly out of the way. The fork hit the ground so hard that sparks flew.

The Flicker drew his towel back and launched an enormous flick, but Gran rolled quickly back the other way. A chunk of cement flew up and whistled past Zack's ears.

"You chuckleheads!" said Gran as the Forker and the Flicker prepared to mount a double attack. "It's me, Mabel! Don't you recognize your old leader?"

The Forker, momentarily confused, stopped and stared at her.

Zack watched as a light dawned in his eyes . . . and then set again.

"More zombie-butt trickery!" yelled the Forker, preparing to plunge again.

"No!" said the Flicker, reaching out to stop him. "Hold your fork!"

But the Flicker was too late.

The Forker forked.

"Watch out, Gran!" yelled Zack.

Gran tried to roll out of the way, but this time she wasn't fast enough. The massive fork pierced the ground, catching the hem of her dress and pinning her to the ground. Meanwhile the Forker drew a handful of smaller forks from his belt and hurled them toward Zack and Eleanor — surrounding them in a circular prison of forks.

Then the Forker raised his fork high above his head.

"No!" said the Flicker, flicking his towel and sending the Forker's fork flying.

The Forker pulled another fork from his belt. "You shouldn't have done that," he said, looking angrily at the Flicker. "You — "

"Mind your language!" warned Gran.

The Forker froze, mid-fork. "Pincher?" he said.

"Yes!" she said with relief. "It's been a long time. Don't you recognize me?"

"The Pincher died many years ago," said the Forker, raising his fork high above his head. "You are a zombie and to honor the name of Mabel Freeman, it is my sacred duty to kill you!"

"She's *not* a zombie!" said the Flicker. "Check her butt!"

The Forker prodded Gran's backside with his fork.

"Hey!" said Gran. "Put a hole in my false butt and I'll pinch your head so hard it will pop!"

That seemed to be all the proof the Forker needed. "It really *is* you!" said the Forker, using the prongs of his fork to scratch his head. "But how in the univarse —"

"Language!" said Gran.

"Definitely the same old Pincher!" laughed the Flicker. "We thought you died in a butt-blitz."

"No," said Gran. "There was no butt-blitz. My disappearance was part of a secret relocation scheme organized by the FBBI for my own safety."

"But why didn't you tell us?" said the Flicker.

"I couldn't!" Gran replied. "To do so would have put both myself and you in extreme danger. It was horrible, I know, but I didn't want you at the mercy of ruthless butts who would be able to torture the information out of you. It was better that you didn't know. Now unfork me this instant!"

The Forker pulled his fork out of Gran's sleeve.

"You'll have to excuse the Forker," said the Flicker. "But he's getting old and his eyesight isn't what it used to be."

"My hearing is fine!" said the Forker.

"His hearing's not too good, either," said the Flicker. "He's getting old."

"I may be getting a cold," said the Forker, spinning a fork like a gunslinger and then sliding it back into his belt, "but I've forked more butts than you've flicked this morning."

"Rubbish," said the Flicker, twirling a towel. "I've flicked more butts than you've forked!"

"Stop your bickering," said Gran. "We've got butts to fight!"

"Watch out behind you!" shouted Eleanor. "That butt has re-formed!"

The Forker and the Flicker spun around.

"I'll get it!" they both yelled, elbowing and pushing each other.

But before they could sort themselves out, the butt leaped at them, knocking them both over.

Gran jumped up and threw herself on top of the butt. It jumped into the air trying desperately to buck her off but she clung tight. Then, in the most spectacular display of pinching prowess Zack had ever seen, Gran pinched it into two halves, the two halves into quarters, and then the quarters into eighths. Her fingers were just a blur as she shredded the butt into smaller and smaller pieces.

"Is there a water faucet around here?" said Gran when she'd finished, holding her hands out in front of her.

"Over there," said the Flicker.

Gran went over to the tap and began washing her hands.

"Hey," said Zack, rattling the forks like the bars of a cage. "What about us?"

The Forker pulled one of the forks out of the ground and Zack and Eleanor squeezed through the gap.

"Sorry about that," he said, holding out his hand. "I'm the Forker!"

Zack shook his hand. "It's an honor to meet you. My name's Zack," he said.

Eleanor stepped forward. "And I'm Eleanor," she said.

The Forker studied her closely. "You're Silas Sterne's little girl, aren't you?"

"I'm not a little girl," said Eleanor. "I'm a butt-fighter."

"Sorry," said the Forker. "No offense intended. Any friend of Mabel Freeman is a friend of mine," he said offering her an enormous dirt-encrusted hand.

"And mine," said the Flicker. "Pardon me if I don't shake your hands, but I've only just washed them."

"Where's everybody else?" called Gran, still scrubbing her hands under the faucet as if preparing for an operation. "Have they all been zombie-buttified?"

"No," said the Forker. "We're the only two left. The rest have all passed on to the great butt-fight in the sky.

The Poker, the Splitter, the Slammer, the Bruiser, the Tickler, the Scalder, the Brander, the Plugger, the Torcher, the Biter, and the Detonator . . . all gone."

"It's a quiet life," said the Flicker, cracking the end of his towel against the zombie butt that had reassembled yet again. "Well, it was until now."

"Stop complaining," said the Forker. "It sure beats sitting around talking about the good old days! We all have to go out sooner or later and what better way to go than in the butt-fight of all butt-fights! I'm only sorry those zombie butts wrecked my garden!"

"I'm only sorry that we're going to lose!" said the Forker.

"We haven't lost yet, soldier!" said Gran, grabbing him by the collar and lifting him up to her face. "Or my name's not the Pincher!"

● ● ●

As Gran spoke, the sky darkened.

Zack looked up.

Coming toward them was a fresh swarm of zombie butts.

"Assume attack positions!" yelled the Forker, crouching low with a fork in each hand. The Flicker leaped into place beside him, twirling a towel covered in brown stains.

But Gran stepped in front of them both.

"You boys go and wash your hands and get ready for dinner," she said. "I'll finish up here."

"But, Pincher!" said the Flicker. "It's too dangerous. You can't hurt them. They don't feel pain!"

"Neither do I," said the Pincher. "Stand back!"

Gran flexed her arms and then, snapping and clicking her clawlike fingers like maracas, she walked forward until she was in the middle of the circling zombie butts.

"I hope she knows what she's doing," said Eleanor.

"Me, too," said Zack.

The butts were close now. So close that Gran could reach out and grab one. Which is exactly what she did.

Zack flinched.

But instead of pinching the butt, as Zack had expected, Gran seized its arms and legs and deftly tied them together. Then she grabbed a second butt and knotted its arms and legs together with the first.

She continued this until she was standing in front of a big pile of wriggling, writhing, trembling, jellylike, knotted-together zombie butts — including the butt that she had previously shredded, which despite her and the Flicker's best efforts had put itself back together and joined in the attack.

Zack applauded, proud of his gran.

Even Eleanor had to nod approvingly.

The Flicker cracked his towel so loudly that it made Zack's ears hurt.

The Forker raised a fork high into the air. "Victory!" he yelled.

But Gran wasn't happy.

"Victory-schmictory!" she said, wiping her brow. "The battle's not over yet, soldier. Those knots won't last forever. We still have to destroy them."

"But how?" asked the Forker.

"The sauna!" said the Flicker. "We can't defeat them by force, but we might be able to sweat them down to nothing."

"Brilliant!" said Gran.

The Forker jabbed a fork into the zombie butt boulder and began pushing it toward the sauna, causing the butts to emit a particularly foul and putrid gas. In fact, it was so horrible that even Zack's butt started coughing and gagging.

"That's absolutely disgusting," it rasped between coughs. "They should be ashamed of themselves!"

Zack pinched his nose.

With each of the Forker's jabs, Zack was reminded yet again that, despite the profession's glamorous image, butt-fighting was a dirty, unpleasant business. He was tempted to turn around and go home . . . until he remembered that he didn't actually have a home to go to. Or a town for that matter. Or even a family.

"Open the door!" shouted the Forker.

The Flicker pulled the heavy wooden door open and was immediately engulfed by a cloud of steam.

"YAH!" yelled the Forker as he forked the butts through the door with one last mighty thrust.

"Language!" said Gran.

The Forker turned around, steam pouring out behind him as he triumphantly raised his fork to the sky.

Zack felt a lot safer than he had for a long time.

But as he watched the Forker forking the air, Zack noticed something moving inside the sauna.

The zombie butts!

They'd broken free of their knots!

And they were heading for the door.

Zack leaped forward and, knocking the Forker flying, slammed his shoulder against the door.

"Good work, Zack," said the Forker, picking himself up off the ground. "I was just about to do that."

Zack peered inside the little square window at the top of the door. The zombie butts were going absolutely nuts. Far from slowing them down and melting them, the heat seemed to be speeding them up.

Zack gulped.

Normal zombie butts were bad enough, but supercharged zombie butts . . . well . . . he shuddered at the thought.

Zack could feel them slamming against the door.

"They're going crazy," he said. "It's not working!"

"Turn up the heat!" said Eleanor.

"It's already up pretty high," said the Flicker.

"Turn it up higher!" said Gran.

The Flicker nodded and adjusted the dial on the temperature unit.

Zack trembled as he watched the butts bounce around the sauna faster and faster until they were just blue-black streaks barely visible through the steam.

The sound of them hitting the walls was deafening. The sauna door was beginning to splinter.

"Higher!" commanded Gran.

"I've got it up higher than it's ever been," said the Flicker, sweating. "It's higher than any human could possibly stand!"

"I hardly have to remind you that those things aren't human," said Gran. "Step aside!"

"No, Pincher," said the Flicker. "If they spontaneously combust, you'll blow us all to Uranus!"

"Language!" said Gran.

"I meant the planet!" said the Flicker.

But Gran wasn't listening. She pushed past him, grabbed the temperature control with her pincer-fingers, and spun it like a top.

"No!" said the Flicker, backing away from the sauna, holding his towel out in front of him like a shield.

"Yes!" said Gran, a strange light shining in her eyes.

Zack was scared. When it came to butt-fighting, Gran didn't seem to have any fear. She was prepared to go all the way. And then even farther.

Both Zack and Eleanor took a step backward.

"Stand your ground, soldiers!" barked Gran. "Tell me what you see!"

Zack was paralyzed.

He was too scared to stay there, but too scared to disobey.

He stayed.

Zombie butts were scary, but right at that moment, his gran was even scarier.

He stepped forward, peered through the window, and was stunned to see the butts lying on the floor in a puddle of blue-black liquid.

"Well?" said Gran.

"They've stopped moving," said Zack. "They're just lying there. It looks like . . . like . . . they're melting."

"Good," said Gran. "That's good."

The Flicker halted his retreat and peeked out from behind his towel.

"Yes, I thought so," he said. "Just as I planned!"

But nobody was taking much notice of the Flicker.

They were all crowded around the window of the sauna watching the zombie butts melt. All of them, that is, except Eleanor. She was looking worried.

"What's the matter, Eleanor?" said Zack.

"I don't know if this is any solution," said Eleanor. "We can't just leave the puddle there. The sauna is going to run out of power sooner or later, and when the puddle cools down there's no guarantee that it won't re-form into one gigantic zombie butt, and then we'll really be in trouble."

Zack began backing away again.

"Don't worry about it," said the Forker. "All we have to do is mop up the mess with one of the Flicker's towels and then we'll take it to the incinerator and burn it."

"No worries!" said the Flicker.

Zack and Eleanor watched as the Flicker grabbed the towel around his waist and began to pull it off.

"Urggh!" they said, covering their eyes.

"Don't worry," said the Flicker. "There are plenty more where this came from!"

Zack peered out from behind his fingers at the Flicker and saw — to his great relief — that the Flicker was wearing another towel underneath the one he had just peeled off. The Flicker bunched up his towel and put it onto the end of the Forker's fork.

"Pincher," said the Forker, "fire up the incinerator. It's behind the greenhouse. We're going to have a good old-fashioned burn-off."

"Right you are," said Gran and she ran off across the croquet lawn toward the greenhouse.

"All right," said the Forker, his hand on the door handle. "Nose plugs, everyone! I'm opening the door!"

Zack barely had time to pull a plug from his belt and snap it onto his nose before he felt a blast of stinking heat.

Through the haze, he saw the Forker entering the sauna and pushing the towel on the end of his fork into the puddle.

"There's too much!" said the Forker, dumping the first towel on the ground behind him. "I need another towel!"

The Flicker peeled a second towel from around his waist and passed it to the Forker.

It wasn't long before the Forker asked for a third towel.

And then a fourth.

"I can't believe you have so many towels wrapped around your waist!" said Zack, amazed.

The Flicker smiled. "A good butt-flicker is always prepared!"

Finally, the mess was all soaked up.

The Forker emerged from the sauna, dug his fork into the pile of towels on the ground and, holding it out in front of him, marched to the incinerator.

Zack, Eleanor, and the Flicker followed him.

When they arrived at the incinerator Gran had a huge blaze going. The flames were leaping high into the air.

The Forker dumped the soggy blue-black mass into the incinerator.

WUMMMMPPPHHH!

The pile of towels exploded into flame and produced clouds of black smoke. It was the most toxic, foul-smelling smoke Zack had ever had the misfortune to encounter.

The stench was worse than the stenches of the midnight butt rally, the Great Windy Desert, the Brown Forest, and Stenchgantor combined.

Zack put his hands to his throat, gasping and choking.

Through his stinging, watering eyes, he saw the others had their hands up to their throats as well.

It was the last thing Zack saw before his vision failed and he fell to the ground.

CHAPTER NINE

The Mutant Maggot Lord

Zack coughed.

His throat was burning.

His lungs were burning.

He opened his eyes.

It was dark.

He tried to sit up, but his wrists and ankles were tied together and it was difficult to move.

Zack didn't know where he was or how long he'd been lying there.

It could have been a few minutes.

It could have been a few days.

He had no idea.

The last thing he could remember was being choked by the black smoke created by the burning zombie butts, but after that, nothing.

On the wall beside him, Zack could see a ladder leading up to a rectangle of light high above. It didn't provide much illumination, but it was enough. As his eyes adjusted to the darkness, Zack was able to make out that he was in an enormous cavernous space filled by a forest of towering concrete pillars. The roots of trees grew through the walls, cracking the concrete and winding across the floor into the pitch-blackness beyond.

Zack shivered.

It reminded him of the drain that he'd been blown into by the cluster butt after the midnight butt rally. The drain where he'd been captured and interrogated by butts.

As far as Zack could now tell, however, he was alone.

And he was frightened.

"Ahh," said a voice. "Awake at last!"

Zack froze.

The voice sent fresh shivers through his body.

Zack peered into the darkness and saw the outlines of two butts coming toward him. One of them was wearing a small paper crown.

There was no mistaking who it was.

The Prince! Leader of Butt Intelligence. And standing next to him was none other than his faithful servant, Maurice.

"You!" said Zack, surprised to say the least. The last time he'd seen the Prince he was being carried off by a wedge-tailed butt-eater. And Maurice had fallen off the side of the buttcano. Neither of them could possibly have survived.

"Yes, it's us!" said the Prince. "Unless I'm very much mistaken, eh, Maurice?"

"Yes," guffawed Maurice at the Prince's little joke. "Unless you're very, very much mistaken!"

Zack tried to pinch his nose to protect himself from the fumes of Maurice's amusement, but remembered he couldn't move his hands. He looked down and saw they were bound with toilet paper.

"What do you think you're doing?" said Zack, struggling to untie his hands. "And what have you done with the others?"

"Relax," said the Prince. "Your friends will be here any moment. They're coming to help save you, just as we knew they would."

As if on cue, they heard Eleanor's voice far above them.

"Zack!" she called. "Zack?"

"Ah . . ." said the Prince. "There they are now . . . right on schedule. That's the one thing I like about butt-fighters. They're very predictable, aren't they, Maurice?"

"Yes, Prince," said Maurice. "Very, very predictable."

"Zack, are you down there?" called Eleanor.

"Call to her," said the Prince. "And no funny business."

"If you think you can buttnap me and use me as bait to catch the others, you're sadly mistaken," said Zack.

"Just call her," said the Prince. "Or else."

"Or else what?" said Zack.

"Or else your butt gets it," said the Prince. He nodded to Maurice.

Maurice yanked hard on a long piece of toilet paper trailing behind him and Zack's butt, attached to the other end, came flying out of the darkness and hit the ground next to Zack.

Zack could see his butt was in a bad way. It had obviously been crying and it had a nasty red rash across both cheeks.

"Help me, Zack," it pleaded. "Please . . . they've got generic toilet paper . . . and they're not afraid to use it!"

"That's enough from you!" said the Prince, shoving a wad of rough-looking toilet paper into Zack's butt to shut it up.

Zack shook his head. Generic toilet paper . . . He knew from experience the Prince and Maurice were ruthless, but he'd never suspected they would stoop this low.

"Zack!" called Gran. "Where are you?"

"Call them," said the Prince.

Zack looked at his trembling butt.

He had no choice.

"I'm here," he called.

"We'll be right down!" yelled Eleanor.

"Good boy," said the Prince as he and Maurice stepped back into the darkness, yanking Zack's butt with them.

"Very, very good boy," said Maurice.

●● ●● ●●

Zack could hear the ladder creaking as Eleanor and the other butt-fighters began their descent.

He felt terrible betraying them like this.

Suddenly there was a loud crash and the butt-fighters landed in a sprawling heap right next to him.

"Get off me, you idiot!" said Eleanor.

"Why don't you get off me, you idiot!" said the Flicker.

"Don't call me an idiot!" said Eleanor.

"I'm not talking to you, you idiot!" said the Flicker. "I'm talking to the Forker."

"I'm not an idiot!" said the Forker.

"Yes, you are," said the Flicker. "You're sitting on my towel, you idiot."

"Language!" said the Pincher.

"Pincher!" said the Forker. "Are you okay?"

"I'm okay," said the Pincher. "But I'd be a lot better if you'd all get off me!"

Eleanor was the first to extract herself.

"Zack!" she said. "We came as soon as we could! The Forker saw you and your butt being buttnapped. He woke us all and we followed you in the butt-mobile. Any idea where the buttnappers are?"

Zack nodded.

"Where?" said Eleanor.

"Right here," said the Prince, stepping forward.

"At your service!" said Maurice.

Eleanor swung around. "You parasites!" she hissed. "I thought you were dead!"

"When the wedge-tailed butt-eater dropped me into its nest I thought I was, too!" said the Prince. "I had ten baby wedge-tailed butt-eaters with razor-sharp beaks snapping around my cheeks . . . but they didn't realize who they were dealing with. And, Maurice, well, I'm not saying he's fat, but he's got enough blubber on him to protect him from a little fall . . . or a big one for that matter."

"Are you saying I'm fat?" said Maurice.

"Yes," said the Prince.

"Thank you," said Maurice. "It's very kind of you to say so. Very, very kind."

"Where in the univarse are we?" said the Forker. "This place stinks!"

"Manners!" said Gran.

"It's quite all right," said the Prince. "No offense taken. Our home may be humble but you are all very welcome, aren't they, Maurice?"

"Very welcome, Prince," said Maurice. "Very, very welcome."

"Who are these butts, anyway?" said the Flicker. "Are they zombies?"

The Prince looked pained. He spat. He looked impatiently at Maurice.

Maurice took his cue. He spat, too.

"Zombie butts?!" exclaimed the Prince. "Now I DO take offense! The lowest of the low!"

"The lowest of the lowest of the low!" intoned Maurice.

"No, they're not zombie butts," said Eleanor, leveling a 4502 Laxative Launcher at them, "just a couple of butts who are about to die."

"Leave it to me," said the Flicker, twirling his towel. "I'll have them flicked in no time."

"No!" said the Forker, fingering the array of forks strapped across his chest. "Let me. I can fork faster than you can flick."

"Oh yeah?" said the Flicker. "I can flick faster than you can fork!"

"Your friends aren't very friendly," said the Prince.

"No," said Eleanor, "and neither am I. Let go of Zack's butt and stand back against the wall."

To Eleanor's — and Zack's — great surprise, the Prince and Maurice did exactly that.

"Thank you," said Eleanor sweetly. "Now, do you have any last words before I blow you both apart?"

"I wouldn't do that if I were you," said the Prince coolly.

"Give me one good reason why I shouldn't," said Eleanor, her finger tightening on the trigger of her butt-gun.

"I can give you a thousand!" said the Prince. "And Maurice can give you a thousand more, can't you, Maurice?"

"Thousands and thousands and thousands!" said Maurice.

"I'm all ears," said Eleanor.

"Then listen," said the Prince. "And you'll hear them."

"What?" said Eleanor, and then she froze.

Curious noises began to echo around them.

In the blackness beyond the small patch of dim light they were standing in, Zack began to make out a vast sea of writhing, glistening shapes slithering toward them.

He knew exactly what they were, he'd seen them before — in the buttcano.

Maggots.

Giant maggots.

But as they drew closer, Zack realized that these giant maggots made the giant maggots he'd seen in the buttcano seem tiny in comparison. These maggots were mutants — some of them three yards long and at least half a yard wide.

Zack and the other butt-fighters shrank back as the mutant maggots crowded around them. They slid in from all sides, completely cutting off any possibility of reaching the access ladder.

"Don't worry," said the Forker, fingering his forks with his forking hand. "I'll have them forked in no time."

"No!" said the Flicker, twirling his towel. "Forking's too good for mutant maggots. Let me flick them!"

"That's not a good idea," said the Prince. "You'd never make it out alive."

"You little fink!" said Eleanor.

"Language!" said Gran. "If you can't say something nice, then it's better not to say anything at all."

"But he *is* a fink!" said Eleanor. "He trapped us!"

"Think of it not so much as a trap as an invitation," said the Prince.

"An invitation for what?" asked the Forker. "To become maggot-food?"

"Oh no," said the Prince.

"Oh no, no, no," said Maurice.

"An invitation to help our master," said the Prince.

"The Great White Butt is dead," said Zack. "Remember the buttcano? The explosion? It's dead!"

"That was our old master," said the Prince, wiping a tear from his eye. "But we have a new master now. And we'd very much like you to meet him. He's *very* eager to meet you, isn't he, Maurice?"

"Oh yes, sir, he is very eager. Very, very eager indeed. Very, very, very, very . . ."

"That will do, Maurice," said the Prince.

"Well, where is he?" asked Eleanor.

"He approaches now," said the Prince, and he turned, bowed, and removed his crown. The others turned to look in the same direction and saw a small figure dragging itself through the maggots toward them.

●● ●● ●●

"What is it?" whispered Eleanor.

"I don't know," said Zack, "but it's giving me the creeps."

Zack glanced across at Mabel's Angels. The Forker had his hand on one of his biggest forks, ready to draw. The Flicker was slowly twirling a towel in each hand. And judging from her smile and her twitching fingers, it was clear that Gran was relishing the prospect of a mutant-maggot pinching spree.

As the figure drew closer, Zack could see that it was completely wrapped in burlap — even its head.

Finally, it stopped and the maggots moved in close, gently rubbing themselves against it.

"Welcome to the Maggotorium!" said the creature in a soft voice. "I am the Maggot Lord. The *Mutant* Maggot Lord. It's very kind of you to come and it's always nice to see old friends."

Zack frowned. Old friends? What did he mean, old friends? He'd never even seen a Maggot Lord before —

especially not a Mutant Maggot Lord — and he'd certainly never been friends with one. And yet, he did have to admit that there was something familiar about his polite and charming manner.

"Get to the point," said Eleanor. "Why are we here?"

"Because I have a proposition for you," said the Mutant Maggot Lord.

"Well, what a coincidence," said Eleanor, "because I've got a proposition for you. Why don't you take your mutant maggots and your little toady butts and shove them right up your mutated . . ."

The Mutant Maggot Lord shuddered.

"Language, young lady!" said Gran.

"Hear me out," said the Mutant Maggot Lord. "That is all I ask."

"All right," said the Forker, gripping his fork so hard that his knuckles were white. "Just get on with it."

"My pleasure," said the Mutant Maggot Lord. "I understand that the planet is currently in the process of being zombie-buttified by zombie butts from Uranus."

"Language!" said Gran.

"I mean the planet, dear lady," said the Mutant Maggot Lord.

"Oh," said Gran. "That's all right then. I thought you meant . . ."

"And conventional butt-fighting methods are useless against them," continued the Mutant Maggot Lord. "Am I correct?"

"Mostly," admitted the Forker. "We managed to melt some . . . but . . ."

The Mutant Maggot Lord finished his sentence for him. "But you're fighting a losing battle, am I right?"

Nobody answered.

"Am I wrong?" demanded the Mutant Maggot Lord again.

"You're right," admitted Gran reluctantly.

"My intelligence is good," said the Mutant Maggot Lord. He reached out a wizened hand — well, at least Zack thought it was a hand — and patted the Prince. "You have served me well."

At the Mutant Maggot Lord's touch, the Prince seemed to go weak at the knees.

"And your point is?" said Eleanor, looking like she was about to be sick.

"I believe we can help one another," said the Mutant Maggot Lord. "I have a vast army of mutant maggots — as you can see — and they have a vast appetite. The Prince and Maurice do their best to procure what road-kill they can, but there is, of course, never enough to go around." He said this sadly, patting the head of one of his maggots as he did so.

"Never enough of what, exactly?" said Eleanor.

"Well," said the Mutant Maggot Lord, "being mag-gots, they need dead flesh." He paused for his words to sink in. "*Lots* of dead flesh."

Eleanor leaned forward, suddenly interested. "Like zombie butts?" she said.

The Mutant Maggot Lord nodded. "They would do very nicely," he said, raising his mutated hand under-neath his burlap shroud to touch his mouth.

The gesture reminded Zack of someone, but he still couldn't think who it could be.

"So what do you want with us?" said Gran. "Why don't you take them up to the surface and let them have their fill?"

"Ah," said the Mutant Maggot Lord, raising a hand to his mouth again. "That's where I have a little problem . . . I mean, *we* have a little problem. You see, my precious babies don't have any legs. It's difficult for them to move around. At least to move around quickly enough to catch zombie butts, that is. What I need is somebody to round up all the zombie butts and bring them down here . . . I'll have my maggots waiting, and I can assure you, it won't take long."

The butt-fighters looked at one another, nodding slowly.

Zack had to admit that the Mutant Maggot Lord's plan made sense — well, at least the sort of sense that made sense in a world that seemed to have stopped making any sense whatsoever.

The Mutant Maggot Lord raised his hand to his mouth and coughed politely. "Well?" he said, "do we have a deal?"

Suddenly Zack clicked his fingers. "I DO know you!" he yelled, finally placing the politeness, the charm, and the constant mouth-touching. "You're . . . the Kisser!"

"The Kisser?" said the Flicker.

"Who's the Kisser?" said Gran.

"A butt-fighter," sneered Zack. "Or should I say, an *ex*-butt-fighter."

"What?" said the Forker. "You mean he kisses butts? That's the most disgusting thing I've ever heard!"

"What are you talking about, Zack?" said Eleanor. "Have you gone mad?"

"Look," said Zack, stepping forward and reaching toward the burlap sack that covered the Mutant Maggot Lord's head. "I'm sure of it."

Suddenly the maggots rose up together, like an army of snakes about to strike.

"NO!" cried the Mutant Maggot Lord, putting his arms over his head. "Not my face. Nobody sees my face. Leave me that much dignity."

"See?" said Zack, holding his hands in the air and backing away, having proved his point. "It *must* be the Kisser. Who else would be so vain?"

"Kisser?!" said Eleanor to the pathetic figure in front of her. "Is it true?"

"I used to be the Kisser," said the Mutant Maggot Lord after a moment's silence. "But not anymore. Not now that I have no lips. Not since you so cruelly abandoned me and left me to die in the brown lake."

Eleanor spat on the ground in front of him. "You've got a nerve," she said. "We didn't abandon you. We tried to help you, but you wouldn't help yourself, you butt-sympathizing traitor!"

"I understand how you must feel," said the Mutant Maggot Lord. "It is true I was guilty of some errors of judgment, but that's all in the past now. The important thing is that I have learned my lesson. And I am eager to make amends."

"But how did you survive?" said Eleanor. "You were pulled into the brown lake by giant maggots. How could anybody survive that?"

"Ah, don't you remember, Eleanor?" said the Mutant Maggot Lord. "They pulled me into the lake out of love, not hunger! You might say they loved me to death. But they also saved me. True, not before the prolonged exposure to the toxic effects of the lake mutated my body, but I survived and apart from losing my good looks — and my lips — am richer for the experience. I have a family now." He turned and stroked the heads of his maggots who were pressing in close all around him.

"Family?" scoffed Eleanor. "You had a family then. They were called the B-team. But you betrayed them. Worse. You tried to kill them. You tried to kill *us*. How do we know you won't do it again?"

"I was confused," said the Mutant Maggot Lord. "What I did was unforgivable, I know. But I've changed."

"You say you've changed," said Eleanor, "but less than an hour ago you buttnapped Zack and his butt and used them to trap us all."

"Would you have come if I'd asked you?" said the Mutant Maggot Lord.

Nobody replied.

"Just as I thought," continued the Mutant Maggot Lord. "Given the circumstances, it was the only way I could get you here. If we don't act quickly, the zombie butts will end up multiplying beyond even what my maggots can consume and we will all perish."

"If you think we're going to cut a deal with you, then you're crazy," said Eleanor. "You've betrayed us before. You'll betray us again!"

"Think about what you're saying, Eleanor," said the Mutant Maggot Lord. "Are you saying you would prefer to watch the entire world laid waste by zombie butts — the atmosphere poisoned by ever-increasing clouds of methane — rather than prevent it with a simple act of forgiveness?"

Eleanor just laughed. "That's rich, coming from you! If you really have changed, prove it by doing the decent thing and letting us all go!"

"But how do I know you'll help me?" said the Mutant Maggot Lord.

"You're just going to have to *trust* us," said Eleanor. "We want to see an end to the zombie butts as much as you do — and maybe your maggot army is the answer — but it's not going to happen if you try to force us. Or trick us. Or deceive us. You've tried that before and look where it's got you. You betrayed our trust, and now you have to earn it back."

The Mutant Maggot Lord was silent.

Zack bit his lip as he stared at the abject figure on the floor in front of him. The Kisser's betrayal of the B-team had cost him dearly. His looks. His body. His lips. And now he was condemned to live underground — a ghost of his former self — with only maggots for company. Mutant maggots. Even though it was all his own fault, it was hard not to feel a little bit sorry for him.

Zack looked at the others.

He could see he was not the only one who felt this

way. Gran was dabbing at her eyes with a handkerchief. The Flicker blew his nose on one of his towels. The Forker, sniffling, reached across to the Flicker's towel and blew his nose on it. Even Zack's butt was blinking back tears.

Eleanor, however, was clearly unmoved.

She stood there, tapping her foot as she waited for the Mutant Maggot Lord's response.

"You're right, Eleanor," the Mutant Maggot Lord finally said in a soft voice. "You're absolutely right. Deceit has got me nowhere." He turned to the Prince and Maurice. "Let the prisoners go," he said.

"But, Master . . ." said the Prince.

"Do as I say," said the Mutant Maggot Lord firmly.

"Yes, Master," said the Prince, unwrapping the toilet paper from Zack's arms and legs, while Maurice removed the leash and the wad of paper from Zack's butt.

"About time, too," said Zack's butt, getting up and joining Zack and the rest of the group.

"So, do I have your word that you will help me?" said the Mutant Maggot Lord.

Eleanor stared at him. "Yes," she said, at last. "You have my word."

Eleanor's response shocked Zack. It was the last thing he'd expected her to say. But he was glad she had said it. He breathed a sigh of relief and smiled.

The Forker smiled.

The Flicker smiled.

Gran smiled.

Eleanor glared at them.

The Mutant Maggot Lord nodded and the maggots

that had closed in around them parted, leaving the way clear for them to climb the ladder back to the surface. "Thank you!" he said. "I won't let you down! Bring the zombie butts to me as soon as you can and you'll see. You won't regret your decision, I promise."

CHAPTER TEN

Hokeypokey

After a long climb, Zack emerged from the drain, which was located at the edge of a large park.

Zack's throat was still sore from the smoke and the stench of methane that permeated the air was making it very difficult to breathe. He looked up at the sky. It was a brilliant blue. There must be an enormous amount of methane in the atmosphere he thought.

Zack shielded his eyes with his hand. He was no genius, but you didn't have to be Einstein to understand the second law of physics, known to butts and buttfighters and schoolchildren throughout the univarse:

Butts + Food = Methane

Only in this case, Zack realized, it was an equation of an even greater magnitude:

Lots of Butts + Lots of Food = Lots of Methane

Just exactly how much methane the zombie butts had produced, Zack had no way of knowing. But they hadn't been here for very long and if the awful stinking haze around them was any indication, it would eventually be more than enough to kill every man, woman, and child on Earth. Not to mention every other living organism as well.

"Looks like we don't have much time," said Zack as Eleanor pulled herself up out of the drain. "Just one question: How do we get them to come back to the Maggotorium with us?"

"Are you kidding?" said Eleanor, helping Gran out. "We're not actually going to help that dirty double-crossing mutant. I only said that to get us out of there!"

"But it could work!" said Gran. "And a promise *is* a promise."

"Not to the Kisser, it's not," said Eleanor. "He was going to kill us!"

"We have no evidence of that," said the Forker, squeezing himself out of the narrow hole with difficulty, "and he *did* let us go."

"He shouldn't have trapped us in the first place!" said Eleanor.

"But his maggot army may be able to help get rid of the zombie butts!" said the Flicker, jumping out after the others. "There's no other way. Even if we could burn them all, we'd choke to death on their fumes!"

"Listen, everybody!" said Eleanor. "Think, think,

THINK! The zombie butts are ZOMBIES. Even if I thought it was a good idea to deal with the Kisser — which I don't — but even if I did, there's no way we could get the zombie butts to do what we want them to do!"

Gran cleared her throat. "I've got a plan," she said.

"What is it?" said Zack.

"Well," said Gran, "why don't we all go back to the butt-mobile, put the kettle on, and have a nice cup of tea?"

"That's ridiculous!" said Eleanor. "We have a code-brown situation here and you're suggesting that we sit down and drink tea? You must have methane madness!"

"Mind your manners, now," said Gran. "A code-brown situation is no excuse for rudeness."

"Well, I for one could sure use a cup," said the Forker.

"Me, too," said the Flicker.

"Me, three," said Zack. "My throat is killing me."

Eleanor shrugged theatrically. "Oh, I just remembered," she said. "I don't have a teapot on the butt-mobile. Or teacups. Or any tea for that matter. And I'm clean out of milk and sugar."

"That's quite all right, soldier," said Gran, lifting up her sweater to reveal a butt-fighter's belt equipped with a teapot, teacups, and three small canisters: the first marked "tea," the second "milk," and the third "sugar." "When you've fought butts for as many years as I have, you learn to pack *all* the essentials."

◉ ◉ ◉

Twenty minutes later, they were all sitting in the butt-mobile sipping English breakfast tea. Even Zack's butt was sipping, although — it must be said — not very elegantly.

"Stop slurping!" said Zack.

"I can't help it," said his butt. "It's too hot."

"Then blow on it," said Zack, and immediately wished he hadn't.

There was pandemonium in the butt-mobile as the butt-fighters fumbled for their nose plugs.

"This is all very pleasant," said Eleanor, after the butt-fighters had finished coughing and gagging and resumed drinking their cups of tea. "But I hardly see how it's helping us fight zombie butts."

"Well I'll be a butt's uncle!" said the Forker who was holding a teacup in one hand and scanning the horizon with a pair of buttoculars in the other. "Would you look at that!"

"What?" said Zack.

"Zombie butts," said the Forker, handing him the buttoculars. "Bigger than I've ever seen them! And one of them's trying to dance!"

Zack looked through the buttoculars at a shopping center parking lot about half a mile away from the butt-mobile. There was a group of the hugest, most enormous zombie butts Zack had ever seen. They were standing in a circle. But as extraordinary as the sight was, what was even more extraordinary was that there was a zombie butt in the middle of the circle, moving its arms and legs in a repetitive, almost rhythmic way.

"It does look like it's dancing," said Zack, handing the buttoculars to the Flicker.

The Flicker nodded and then shook his head. Then he nodded again.

"Let me see," said Gran, taking the buttoculars from the Flicker.

"That's impossible!" said Eleanor. "Have you all got methane madness?"

"Here, see for yourself," said Gran, handing her the buttoculars. "It's dancing, all right."

Eleanor looked and then handed the buttoculars back to the Forker.

"Well?" said Zack.

"I think I must have methane madness, too," said Eleanor.

"It's dancing, all right," said the Forker, watching the butt, "but not as we know it. I could be wrong, but I think that zombie butt is talking to the others."

"Talking?" said Eleanor. "But they're zombies. They can't talk."

The Forker drew his breath in. "I used to keep bees," he said, "and they do a similar sort of thing. That's how they communicate. They use simple repetitive gestures to tell one another where to find food."

"But the zombie butts don't eat food," said Eleanor.

"No," said the Forker. "Not directly. They need a victim to attach themselves to. And judging by the size of those butts, they've outgrown their original hosts and are looking for some bigger ones. You know, this could be the break we've been looking for."

"Are you saying we should go out there and dance for them?" asked Gran.

"Not exactly," said the Forker. "They'd probably try to attach to us. We need a butt."

Zack's butt went pale and almost choked on its tea. "Why are you all looking at me?" it said.

"Relax," said the Forker. "All you'd have to do is to tell them where they can find lots of new victims."

"The maggots?" said Eleanor.

"Yes," said the Forker.

"No way!" said Eleanor, raising her voice. "We're *not* dealing with the Kisser. I thought I made that clear!"

"I understand your reluctance, Eleanor," said the Forker, "and believe me, if I thought we had any other option, I would try it. But we don't."

"Well, don't worry about it because I'm not doing it and that's final," said Zack's butt. "Tell him, Zack."

"He's right," said Zack to the Forker. "It's too dangerous. There's got to be another way."

"It's the ONLY way!" said the Forker. "We know the zombie butts are impervious to forking, flicking, and pinching. There's too many to melt and the smoke is too dangerous. But we might be able to get them to move if we can convince them that there's plenty of fresh hosts waiting for them in the Maggotorium. And the only way we can convince them of that is to send your butt out there and let them know about it."

"But I can't dance!" said Zack's butt, jumping up into Zack's arms for protection.

"Anyone can learn to dance," said the Forker. "It's just a matter of practice. And besides, this is a very simple dance. You can move your arm up and down — like so — I presume?" The Forker moved his arm up and down.

"Yes," said Zack's butt, "of course, but . . ."

"You can turn around, can't you?" said the Forker, turning around. "Like this?"

Zack's butt nodded. "Yes, I can do all that, but . . ."

"Then you can do the dance!" said the Forker.

"You're forgetting one important thing, though," said Zack's butt. "I don't look like a zombie butt any more than you do! I'm pink and they're blue! I'm alive and they're dead!"

"We can fix that with a little buttouflage," said the Forker.

"No!" said Zack's butt. "I won't do it. And that's final!"

"You'll be a hero," said the Flicker.

"You'll save the world!" said Gran.

"You could even be the first butt to be nominated for the Butt Hunters' Hall of Fame," said the Forker.

"On the other hand," said Zack's butt, "I might get zombie-buttified!"

"Not if you do exactly as I tell you," said the Forker.

Zack's butt sighed heavily.

The butt-fighters reached for their nose plugs.

Zack could see the logic in the Forker's suggestion. He spoke quietly to his butt. "If you do this," he said, "I'll give you your very own fluffy pink toilet seat cover."

"And extra-soft toilet tissue?" said his butt.

"*Extra*-extra-soft toilet tissue," said Zack.

"And no smacks ever again?"

Zack hesitated, then agreed. "No smacks."

"Ever?" said his butt.

"Ever," promised Zack.

"And your fingers aren't crossed?" said his butt.

Zack held up his hand and wiggled his fingers.

"Okay," said his butt.

Zack looked at the others. "He'll do it," he said.

"Hang on," said Eleanor. "How do we know that we can trust it to give the zombie butts the right information? Your butt might not be a zombie butt, but it *is* a butt. And not so long ago, it was trying to take over the world. How do we know that it's not going to go out there and just tell them exactly where we are?"

Zack's butt looked hurt. "I guess you'll just have to trust me," it said.

"I'll never trust a butt as long as I live!" said Eleanor.

"You're just saying that because you're jealous," said Zack. "Just because you cut your own butt loose!"

"Butt sympathizer!" said Eleanor, taking a swing at Zack.

"Language *and* manners!" said Gran sharply. "I don't like butts any more than you do, soldier, but let's not forget who the real enemy is here. And let's also not forget that you're a young lady."

Eleanor glared at them all. "Fine," she said. "So let me get this straight. Our plan pretty much consists of relying on a butt-sympathizing traitor who very recently tried to kill an entire team of butt-fighters, a load of mutated maggots who very recently were blocking our escape from the Maggotorium, and a megalomaniac butt who very recently tried to create a buttcano that would kill every human being on Earth. Am I correct?"

"No," said Zack's butt. "I didn't know the buttcano was going to kill everyone . . . that was the Great White Butt's idea . . . it told us that it would just put you out of action for a little while."

"Oh, that's right," said Eleanor. "My mistake. You just wanted to put a butt on the head of every human being on the planet and put their heads where their butts should be."

"I said I was sorry," said Zack's butt. "So did the Kisser."

"Oh, silly me!" said Eleanor, striking her head with the palm of her hand. "I forgot. You said 'sorry'! Well that makes it all right then, doesn't it? Gee! What a good plan! Sounds absolutely foolproof. Wish I'd thought of it myself!"

"Mind your sarcasm!" said Gran. "It may not be the greatest plan in the world, but it's better than nothing. Another cup of tea, anyone?"

Exactly one hour later, Eleanor flew the butt-mobile toward the center of Mabeltown. Normally she would have done all she could to conceal their arrival, but this time she flew low and revved the engines loudly to make sure they were well noticed.

"Oh no," said Zack as he looked out of the window at the scene below them.

"What is it?" said Zack's butt, jumping up onto his lap.

"Look," said Zack.

The normally quiet shopping strip was filled with zombies. Zombies staggering around with enormous butts. Huge butts. They were at least three times as big as the butts that had originally landed. Zack was amazed that the zombies could walk at all, and in fact, as he looked closer, he discovered that many of them had simply collapsed face-first under their own weight. Others were sitting up against shop windows holding their stomachs as if they'd eaten too much Christmas dinner. Those that could still stagger appeared to be intent on eating nonstop. They were filling their faces with food — or whatever they could get their hands on. A crowd of zombies were fighting over the contents of a garbage can. Others — clearly even more desperate — were on their knees licking the road.

"This is terrible," said the Forker, standing behind Zack.

"There's nothing left," said the Flicker.

"But they can't stop eating," said Gran. "Not while the butts are attached."

When Eleanor was sure that every scrounging zombie and zombie butt in the vicinity was aware that they were there, she landed. There was a soft bump as the butt-mobile came to rest. Zack was nervously applying his butt's buttouflage with blue eye shadow and mascara.

"Watch out for my eye!" said his butt. "That stuff stings!"

"Sorry," said Zack. "But you keep moving!"

"I'm only doing what the Forker is telling me to do!" said Zack's butt.

"Okay, let's go over it one more time," said the Forker.

"I KNOW it already!" said Zack's butt.

"Humor me," said the Forker.

Zack's butt sighed and repeated what the Forker had taught him. "I let them know there's a huge supply of maggot-hosts, so I wriggle like a maggot."

"Shouldn't be too hard," said Eleanor under her breath.

"What did you say?" said Zack's butt.

"Nothing," said Eleanor.

"Ignore her," said the Forker. "Do the maggot!"

Zack's butt self-consciously put its arms in the air and wriggled and swayed like a belly dancer.

Zack tried to stifle a nervous laugh.

"Shut up!" said his butt. "I'd like to see you do better."

Zack shook his head. "I couldn't," he said. He wasn't lying, either. Not only had he failed his Junior Butt-fighters' League entrance exam three times, he'd also embarrassed himself at school dance classes. It wasn't that he didn't *want* to dance, it's that he just had no idea *how* to dance. He knew that the girls in the class dreaded being his partner. He would step too fast, or too slow, or simply step on their toes. He'd drop them when he was supposed to catch them. When it came to dancing, he was a one-man walking disaster area. Except for the hokeypokey. He was very good at the hokeypokey. But then, that wasn't saying much. A two-year-old could dance the hokeypokey.

Zack's butt finished its impression of a maggot.

"Good!" said the Forker. "Now, where is the Maggotorium? Show me the direction."

"It's northeast of the town, so I point this way," said Zack's butt, extending its arm toward the back of the butt-mobile.

"No!" said the Forker. "That's southwest! Come on! We've been over and over this!"

"Okay, okay," said Zack's butt pointing toward the front of the butt-mobile. "Northeast! There . . . how's that?"

"Better," said the Forker, biting his lip. "And how far?"

"It's two miles from the center of town to the Maggotorium," said Zack's butt, pumping its right arm in the air, "so I shake my arm twice."

The Forker nodded uncertainly. "Okay," he said. "Do you want to go through it one more time?"

"NO!" said Zack's butt, jumping up from its seat and pushing Zack's hand away. "And no more makeup, either. I don't want to look like a sissy."

"Uh-oh," said Eleanor. "Looks like we've got company."

Zack looked out the window.

Although they'd been stationary for only a few minutes the butt-mobile was completely surrounded — as far as they could see — by zombies and zombie butts.

"I sure hope this works," said Eleanor.

"Me, too," said Zack's butt, gulping, as it prepared to leave the butt-mobile.

Gran saluted Zack's butt. "It's a brave thing you're doing, soldier!" she said.

Zack shook his butt's hand. "Good luck," he said. "May your butt be with you."

"I *am* a butt, you idiot," said Zack's butt, climbing the hatch ladder.

"Don't forget that it's northeast!" called out the Forker. "Not southwest."

"No worries!" said Zack's butt. "Not southwest . . . it's northeast!" It pointed to the southwest again.

"NO!" yelled the Forker. "It's — "

"Just kidding," said Zack's butt and it disappeared out of the hatch.

Zack watched nervously through the windshield as his butt climbed out onto the nose of the butt-mobile.

The zombies and zombie butts surged in closer.

Zack's butt started to do the moves the Forker had taught it.

It wriggled.

It pointed.

It shook its right arm twice.

The zombies and zombie butts watched it closely, without moving, while Zack's butt did the moves over and over and over again.

And then they attacked.

Zombie butts flew through the air, knocking Zack's butt over. It grabbed onto the side of the butt-mobile and held on tightly as the zombies tried to pull it down into the crowd.

"I should have known this would happen!" screamed Eleanor, desperately trying to power up the butt-mobile.

"I can't understand it," said the Forker. "He did it exactly like I taught him . . ."

Zack looked at his butt. All the color had drained from it. It was terrified.

"I have to go and save my butt!" yelled Zack.

"Have you got methane madness?" said Eleanor. "You'll be zombie-buttified for sure!"

Zack stopped. How was he going to save his butt?

He hadn't learned the dance. And it didn't work anyway. And even if he *had* learned it — which he hadn't — and even if it *did* work — which it didn't — he couldn't dance. Except for the hokeypokey, of course . . .

But that was it!

The Blind Butt-feeler had told him to do the hokeypokey, and that he would know when to do it. And if there was any time to do the hokeypokey, it was right now.

"I'm going to do the hokeypokey!" said Zack.

"You definitely *have* got methane madness," said Eleanor.

But Zack was already halfway out of the butt-mobile.

Outside the air was rancid with zombie butt stench. It was almost as bad as the black smoke. Zack could hardly breathe.

"Zack," called his butt. "Help me!"

"Okay!" he said to his butt. "But you have to do exactly what I tell you to!"

"You're the boss," said his shaking butt.

"Put your left foot in," said Zack, putting his left foot in. His butt followed.

"Now put your left foot out," said Zack, putting his left foot out.

Zack watched as his butt copied. He also noted that quite a few of the zombies were copying as well.

"Now put your left foot in and shake it all about," said Zack.

But then his butt stopped. "What's this all about?" it said.

"Just look out there," said Zack, "and you'll see!"

Zack and his butt looked, and to their amazement, they saw that every single zombie butt had abandoned its human host and was doing the hokeypokey. The dance had a strange hypnotic power over them.

"See?" said Zack, "that's what it's all about!" and he clapped his hands twice.

"Oh!" said his butt, clapping its hands as well. "I get it!"

"Let's go!" cried Zack, jumping down onto the ground and hokeypokeying his way through the crowd in the direction of the Maggotorium.

He looked behind him and to his great relief saw that, along with his own butt, the entire hokeypokeying zombie-butt population of Mabeltown was following him.

CHAPTER ELEVEN

The Great
White Butt

Meanwhile, back on Uranus, the long eighty-four Earth-year orbit of the sun dragged on.

The sun was visible from Uranus, but only a fraction of the massive nuclear furnace's light reached the planet's surface. And even less reached James and Judi at the bottom of the crater.

Judi and James looked at each other.

They'd been in plenty of serious situations together before, but none quite as serious as this.

Standing on the Great White Butt at the bottom of a hole on a hostile planet on the far side of the solar system took the meaning of "serious situation" to a whole new level.

A *serious* new level.

But did they panic?

No.

James and Judi Freeman were professionals. They simply analyzed their situation logically . . . carefully weighing the positives and the negatives in an attempt to find a solution.

"All right," said James. "This is the situation as I see it. We're standing on the Great White Butt at the bottom of a hole on a hostile planet on the far side of the solar system."

Judi nodded. James continued.

"And the sides of the hole are too slippery and unstable to climb and it's two hundred forty degrees below zero and at night it's going to get even colder and we don't have any blankets, food, or water. I think that pretty much sums up the positives."

"You mean there are negatives?" said Judi, feigning surprise.

"Yes, I'm afraid so," said James. "But only two."

"What are they?" said Judi.

"Well," said James, his eyes suddenly widening into twin saucers of horror, "number one, WE'RE DOOMED, and number two, WE'RE GOING TO DIE!!!"

Judi just laughed.

"Why are you laughing?" said James. "This is serious! Seriously serious!"

"Really, James," she said, "I think you're being a little overdramatic. I don't think the situation is quite as bad as you make it sound."

"How could it not be?" he said.

Judi smiled. "You said we couldn't climb out, right?"

"That's right," said James. "It's impossible."

"But there's nothing to stop us from jumping, is there?" said Judi.

"Huh?" said James.

Judi smiled and pushed the Great White Butt's hide with her toe. "Look at this," she said. "It's hard on top, but there's a lot of blubber underneath."

"So?" said James.

"So," said Judi. "Blubber is like rubber. And our bodies currently weigh more than four times their normal weight. This extra weight should be more than enough to allow us to turn the Great White Butt into a giant buttpoline, which — if my calculations are correct — will allow us to bounce out of the crater to safety."

Judi was beaming with the brilliance of her idea.

James studied her closely. "I think you might have methane madness," he said.

"No, I haven't!" said Judi. "Watch."

She steadied herself on the wobbly surface of the Great White Butt and started to bounce. Small cautious bounces at first, which gradually led into bigger and more daring jumps.

"Judi," said James, breaking into a broad grin, "you're a genius!"

He started bouncing as well, turning his arms in tight circles like he used to when he jumped on his bed as a little boy back on Earth.

Within moments, James's and Judi's bounces were truly awesome, sending them many hundreds of yards upward — and so deep — that it looked like they were bungee-jumping with an invisible bungee cord.

"I haven't had so much fun in years!" said James into his headset as he shot up past Judi.

"Me, neither," replied Judi as she hurtled back down toward the Great White Butt's rubbery hide.

But just before she touched down for her next bounce, she noticed the Great White Butt begin to stir.

"James!" she said. "It's moving!"

Suddenly an unearthly noise filled the crater. It was hard to say what it was exactly — something between a shriek and a war cry — but whatever it was, it filled James and Judi with a strange nameless dread.

"Uh-oh. Our bouncing must have revived it!" said James. "Put everything you've got into your next bounce. We've got to reach the top of the crater and get out of here before it wakes up completely!"

Judi hit the Great White Butt and used her powerful legs to take off with incredible force. She stretched her hands above her head, put her palms together, and shot out of the top of the crater like a human torpedo. With a squelch, she landed headfirst on the boggy surface of Uranus.

Inspired by Judi's success, James tried the same maneuver, but as he attempted to bounce, the damaged hide of the Great White Butt shifted again and he hit a deep dimple that absorbed much of the force of his jump. He shot up, but only managed to draw level with the top of the hole. He whipped a toilet brush out of his belt and tried to drive it deep into the side of the crater, but the Uranusian gravity was too strong. It started pulling him back down before he could get the toilet brush properly anchored.

Just as James was beginning to think that he was

doomed and was going to die after all, he heard another earsplitting roar of pain and fury, and a huge blast of gas from below picked him up, carried him out of the crater, and dumped him right beside Judi, who had just extracted her head from the Uranusian bog.

"Aaagghhh!" yelled James, putting his arms over his head. "A bog monster! Don't hurt me!"

"It's just me, you idiot," said Judi, wiping the brown sludge off her space helmet.

James relaxed. "Of course," he said, trying to laugh it off. "I knew that. Just kidding!"

Judi laughed as well.

"Told you there was nothing to worry about," said James.

"Come on," said Judi. "We don't have a moment to lose."

James nodded. He climbed off Judi. Then his face darkened. "Uh-oh," he said.

"What?" said Judi.

But James couldn't speak.

Judi turned to see the most terrifying sight of her entire life.

Hovering above the crater, borne aloft by its own poisonous fumes, was the Great White Butt.

⚫⚫ ⚫⚫ ⚫⚫

Judi looked at James.

James looked at Judi.

"We're doomed and we're going to die!" yelled Judi.

"No we're not!" said James. "RUN!"

"We can't run!" said Judi.

"THEN CRAWL!" said James. "And whatever you do, don't look back!"

They started crawling.

Crawling through the brown muck at a sickeningly slow pace.

The Great White Butt roared.

James and Judi Freeman felt its hot wind blasting them from behind. They could feel the sludge vibrating around them. Judi turned to look at their pursuer.

"Don't look back!" yelled James. "Keep your eyes on the butt-mobile!"

Judi nodded dumbly.

She appreciated James's efforts, but she knew it was useless. They might as well accept the facts of their situation, and the facts of their situation were that they were doomed and they were going to die.

They would never see Earth again.

They would never see their son again.

Judi cried as she crawled.

Of all the rotten bad butt-fighting luck! They'd managed to survive more than twenty years of every dangerous butt and butt-fighting dilemma imaginable . . . until now, anyway.

But somehow, miraculously, Judi saw through her tears that they were getting closer to the butt-mobile. Either that, or the butt-mobile was getting closer to them. But then, so was the Great White Butt.

"Not far now," said James. "Keep crawling!"

Judi summoned the last reserves of her strength and crawled with all her might.

The next thing she knew — and this *had* to be a miracle — she found her brown, sludge-covered hand clutching the ladder that led up the side of the butt-mobile.

She saw James's boot disappearing over the top.

There was still hope!

Despite the powerful gravity pulling her backward, Judi followed him up and was about to drop down into the hatch when she turned around and saw the Great White Butt . . . halfway between the crater and the butt-mobile.

Judi dropped down, sealed the hatch, and yelled at James to gun it.

James, who needed no encouragement, was already in the pilot's seat stamping violently on the thruster pedal.

But the butt-mobile was struggling.

Its engine — an X-9000 bran-assisted bowel-action turbo-thruster, which, while powerful enough in its day, had never been designed with the crippling demands of interplanetary travel in mind — was having trouble getting sufficient thrust to break away from the powerful Uranusian gravity. The fact that it was half-buried in sludge was not helping.

James slammed the steering wheel in frustration. "It's stuck!" he yelled.

Then he looked out of the windshield.

But there was nothing to see but the vast glowing whiteness of the Great White Butt.

James cried out and then went rigid with fear.

"James?" said Judi, running up to the cockpit.

She saw the butt and drew in her breath.

She saw James. He was sitting in his seat, completely frozen. Staring straight ahead of him.

Judi waved her hand in front of his eyes. "James!" she said. "Snap out of it!"

But James's only response was to turn and look at her as if she were a stranger.

"James Freeman!" she yelled, grabbing him by the shoulders and shaking him violently. "Don't do this to me! You can't give up now! Don't leave me here alone!"

But James just stared at her.

Judi stared at him, horrified. Her shoulders slumped and she sighed heavily. So this was how it would end for them. Any moment now the Great White Butt would huff and puff and blow the butt-mobile apart.

Then she noticed a light flashing on the control panel in front of her.

She focused on it. It was the special buttmergency recall lamp. She smiled at the irony. There was nothing she would rather have done in the entire univarse than return home at that moment, and no possible way that she could.

She pushed the button. A small computer screen popped up. Judi read the message:

TO JAMES FREEMAN AND JUDI FREEMAN, please come back immediately. Earth is being taken over by zombie butts from Uranus.
Love, ZACK FREEMAN (your son).
P.S. The Great White Butt is dead! I

**harpooned it and Silas Sterne nominated
me for the Butt Hunters' Hall of Fame.
P.P.S. Gran told me everything.**

The words hit Judi with as much force as if a ton of toilet paper rolls had just been dropped on her head.

Not only was the message completely confounding, it couldn't possibly be true.

First, Zack was no butt-fighter. After all, he couldn't even pass the Junior Butt-fighters' entrance exam. He'd failed three times.

And second, the Great White Butt was definitely not dead.

But then, it had definitely been wounded. And it definitely wouldn't be the first time that the Great White Butt had managed to cheat death.

Judi bit her lip as she read the message again.

Maybe it was true.

Maybe, when it came to butt-fighting, Zack was a late bloomer.

Only one thing was certain.

She couldn't give up now.

While she was powerless to stop the zombie butt invasion, she could at least attempt to finish what her son had started . . . she owed him that much.

Judi patted her dazed husband gently on the shoulder. As she looked at him, she remembered the many dangerous — and wonderful — times they'd had together. She blinked back a tear, left the cockpit, and armed herself with a 370TZ Constipator — the biggest and meanest butt-gun they carried. It was like arming

yourself with a needle against a charging elephant —
she knew that — but it was all she had and she was determined to make the most of it. She was a butt-fighter.
And she had taken the sacred butt-fighter's oath.

With a steely look in her eye she climbed the ladder,
released the hatch door, and went outside.

As Judi climbed onto the roof, she gasped with sheer terror at being so close to the Great White Butt. She remembered her mentor and teacher, Silas Sterne, once
telling her that to control his fear he used to remember
this simple fact: "The largest dinosaur that ever walked
the Earth had a brain the size of a peanut — the largest
butt has even less."

Still, it was a daunting sight and the stench emanating from it made her feel nauseated and light-headed.

But no less courageous.

"Prepare to die!" she announced, lifting the heavy
gun up onto her shoulder, squinting against the Great
White Butt's brightness.

But the Great White Butt just laughed.

The gale of gas blew the 370TZ Constipator out of
Judi's hand, over the edge of the butt-mobile and down
into the brown sludge of Uranus.

Judy looked at her empty hands in disbelief.

"Didn't they teach you anything in school?" said the
Great White Butt. "I am the GREAT WHITE BUTT . . . indestructible and immortal!"

Judi smiled bravely. "And didn't they teach you anything in school about personal hygiene?" she said. "You don't look that great or white to me. Look at yourself! You're sad, pathetic, filthy, and you're missing most of the skin from your right cheek."

"Nobody insults the Great White Butt!" it announced angrily.

"Wrong!" said Judi. "I just did."

"I meant nobody insults the Great White Butt . . . and lives!" it said.

"Wrong again," said Judi, searching the pockets of her spacesuit for her perfume bomb. "My son shot a harpoon into you . . . and he's still alive!"

The Great White Butt visibly brightened. So much so that Judi had to shield her eyes.

"Not for much longer," it said. "But now I feel refreshed and revived by the methane. First I will kill you, and then I'm going to return to Earth to kill your son and take over the world. Any last words?"

Judi, still searching for the perfume bomb, desperately tried to play for time.

"You'll never succeed," she said. "You're too late! The Earth has been invaded by zombie butts created by your collision with this planet!"

"What wonderful news!" said the Great White Butt, brightening again. "That was, of course, exactly my plan. By now my Uranusian zombie butts will have had plenty of time to buttinate the earth and I can now return and take over. So it's all worked out rather well, don't you think?"

"Not so fast, Fatso," said James Freeman, appearing on top of the butt-mobile, a butt-gun in his hands.

"Ah!" said the Great White Butt. "Zack Freeman's father, I presume?"

James nodded.

"This must be my lucky day!" said the Great White Butt. "It started off badly, but it's turned out surprisingly well."

"Well, it just took a turn for the worse!" said James Freeman, pulling the trigger of a series 9000 nail-gun.

But the Great White Butt just laughed as the nails bounced off it. "Stop it," it said. "That tickles."

James threw down the nail-gun in disgust and put up his fists. "Come and fight like a man!" he said.

"But I'm not a man," said the Great White Butt. "I'm a butt!"

"And a very smelly one," said James.

"Thanks," said the Great White Butt as it puffed itself up and prepared to gas the tiny figures standing on the nose of their butt-mobile. "It's very kind of you to say so, but flattery will get you nowhere. And now . . . YOU DIE!"

"No," said Judi, her fingers closing on the perfume bomb. "You do."

Judi pulled the pin of the perfume bomb, counted silently to three, and threw it at the Great White Butt.

But as she did so, the Great White Butt let fly with the most deadly poisonous blast of gas it had ever discharged in its entire life.

There was an enormous explosion as the putrid gas and the fragrant perfume collided . . . and then silence.

CHAPTER TWELVE

Zombie Butt Feast

Zack and his butt hokeyed.

Zack and his butt pokeyed.

Zack and his butt hokeypokeyed down what was left of the main street, on to the road that led out of Mabeltown and toward the Maggotorium, leading a vast conga line of hokeypokeying zombie butts.

"You do the hokeypokey and you turn around . . ." sang Zack at the top of his voice. The zombie butts all turned around. "And that's what it's all about!" Zack clapped his hands twice and the zombie butts all did the same . . . all the way back down the line.

"I'm sick of the hokeypokey!" said Zack's butt, as they launched into the beginning of the whole song and dance again.

"We can't stop now," whispered Zack. "If we do, they could turn on us. We'll end up zombie-buttified quicker than you can say 'zombie-buttification.'"

Zack began the next verse, ignoring his butt's loud sigh.

They hokeyed.

They pokeyed.

They turned around — all the while gaining dozens of fresh zombie butts as they abandoned their hosts to join in the dance.

🍩 🍩 🍩

As Zack hokeypokeyed up toward the entrance to the Maggotorium, he saw Gran, Eleanor, the Forker, and the Flicker forming a guard of honor beside the buttmobile.

Eleanor smiled at Zack. "I didn't know you could dance," she said.

"Just the hokeypokey," shrugged Zack, self-consciously.

"Nice footwork, soldiers," said Gran.

"Good going, Zack!" yelled the Flicker, "See? I told you it would work!" said the Forker, raising his fork in the air.

"Your 'instructions' were wrong," said Zack's butt. "They almost got me killed!"

"Nobody's perfect," said the Forker.

"You're right about that," said Zack's butt, lifting its leg and burping as it hokeypokeyed past the Forker.

The Forker, gagging and choking, waved his fork at Zack's butt.

Meanwhile Zack had reached the manhole that led down to the Maggotorium and was lowering himself down the ladder, hokeypokeying all the while — which is no easy feat when you're trying to climb down a ladder. Zack's butt hokeypokeyed quickly down after him.

The hokeypokeying zombie butts followed obediently. They, however, were too big and clumsy to climb down ladders and do the hokeypokey at the same time. Most of the zombie butts ended up plummeting downward and bouncing all over the Maggotorium like beach balls.

"What do we do now?" said Zack's butt, trying to shield itself from the zombie butts crashing down all around them.

"Get as far away from the ladder as possible and just keep doing the hokeypokey!" said Zack. "If we stop doing it, then they'll stop doing it and then we'll *really* be in trouble."

Zack and his butt hokeypokeyed as far into the Maggotorium as the dim light allowed.

Sure enough, despite the shock of the fall, the bruised and dazed zombie butts continued to be mesmerized by the hokeypokey.

"I'm *really* sick of the hokeypokey now," said Zack's butt as it and Zack danced in front of the hokeypokeying army of zombie butts. "How much longer do we have to do this?"

"Not much longer," said Zack, turning around searching in the gloom for the Mutant Maggot Lord's army of giant mutant maggots. "We're just waiting for the mutant maggots."

Zack's butt looked behind them into the gloom. "Where are they, anyway?"

"Good question," said Eleanor, hokeypokeying her way through the zombie butts with the Forker, the Flicker, and the Pincher up to where Zack and his butt were dancing. "And where's the Mutant Maggot Lord? I knew we shouldn't have trusted him. It's a trick! He's led us all into another trap! The only feast around here is going to be us, and meanwhile, with the zombie butts safely tucked away down here, he'll take over with his mutated maggots. How could we all have been so dumb?"

"You can't help it," said a haughty voice from the darkness behind them. "You are only humans after all, aren't they, Maurice?"

"Oh yes, Master, that is unfortunately so," said Maurice.

The Prince and Maurice shuffled forward, eyeing the zombie butts nervously.

"Where are the mutant maggots, you little punks?" said the Flicker.

"Language!" said Gran.

"And where is the great Mutant Maggot Lord?" said the Flicker. "He said he'd be here."

"And I am," said the Mutant Maggot Lord, dragging his rag-covered form out of the darkness toward them. "What a pity I can't join in your little dance. It looks like such fun."

"We've kept our part of the deal," said Zack, ignoring the Mutant Maggot Lord's sarcasm. "Now you keep yours."

"But of course!" said the Mutant Maggot Lord. "I simply took the precaution of keeping my mutant maggot army hidden. I didn't want the feasting to start before *all* of the zombie butts were inside."

The Mutant Maggot Lord clicked his fingers.

Zack shivered as the Maggotorium filled with the eerie sound of thousands of mutant maggots dragging themselves across the Maggotorium floor.

"Ah, my lovely girls and boys," whispered the Mutant Maggot Lord. "I have a wonderful surprise for you."

Zack watched as the mutant maggots formed a huge white wall in front of the zombie butts.

"Block the exit!" said the Mutant Maggot Lord to the Prince and Maurice. "Nobody . . . no zombie butt — and no mutant maggot — leaves until this is over."

"I'll just be going then, shall I?" said Zack's butt. "After all, I don't technically fit into any of those categories and . . ."

"Shut up," said the Mutant Maggot Lord.

"Language!" said Gran.

"I beg your pardon," said the Mutant Maggot Lord. "Now shut up and keep dancing."

The tone of the Mutant Maggot Lord's voice alarmed Zack. He looked up over his shoulder. The maggots rose high above him. One dribbled a long sticky strand of saliva onto his shoulder.

"Gross!" said Zack. "Maggot-spit!"

"Let the feast begin!" commanded the Mutant Maggot Lord.

Zack, his butt, and the other butt-fighters dived for cover behind the two closest concrete pillars as the white wave of maggots advanced toward the helplessly hokeypokeying zombie butts.

Zack closed his eyes. He'd seen the mutant maggots in action back in the buttcano, and it hadn't been pretty. The zombie butts didn't stand a chance.

But when Zack opened his eyes again, he saw to his surprise that the mutant maggots hadn't eaten a single zombie butt.

"What are you waiting for, my darlings?" yelled the Mutant Maggot Lord. "Eat to your heart's content!"

But the mutant maggots would not start eating. They shrank from the zombie butts, who, slowly waking from the spell of the hokeypokey were now advancing on the maggots.

"What's happening, Kisser?" said Eleanor. "You said your mutant maggots would eat them! If they don't hurry up, they're going to be zombie-buttified and then we'll all be in for it."

"I don't understand," said the Mutant Maggot Lord. "They are not usually fussy eaters. But perhaps even a mutant maggot will not stoop so low as to eat a zombie butt from Uranus."

"Language," said Gran.

"I meant the planet," said the Mutant Maggot Lord.

"You mutant!" screamed Eleanor.

"I'm sorry," said the Mutant Maggot Lord sadly. "It seems that I have led you here under false pretenses. My mutant maggot army cannot save the world after all."

Zack was dumbstruck.

The words *cannot save the world* echoed in his brain.

And then it hit him.

Of course the mutant maggot army couldn't save the world.

There was only one thing that could do that. The Blind Butt-feeler had made that perfectly clear.

Eleanor moved toward the Mutant Maggot Lord, her face contorted with rage. "I KNEW it!" she snarled as she advanced on him with her hands in full smacking position.

"NO!" yelled Zack. "It's not his fault!"

Eleanor glared at Zack. "EVERYTHING'S his fault!" she said.

"Not the fact that maggots won't eat zombie butts from Uranus, though," said Zack, drawing his bottle of ketchup from his belt. "At least, not without ketchup!"

Holding the bottle in both hands, Zack pointed it at the zombie butts and squeezed as hard as he could. Ketchup flew across the Maggotorium and splattered against a number of the zombie butts in the front row.

The effect was as quick as it was terrifying.

Invigorated by the intoxicating smell of freshly squeezed ketchup, the mutant maggots struck.

They surged forward, tearing and chomping the ketchup–covered zombie butts to shreds.

Zack squeezed the ketchup bottle again and again until there was no more ketchup left to squeeze.

But it didn't matter.

The mutant maggots had worked themselves into such a frenzy that every last zombie butt was finally devoured, whether it had ketchup on it or not.

The Maggotorium grew quiet as the mutant maggots retreated into the gloom to digest their meal.

"It's over," said Zack. "We did it!"

"No," said Eleanor. "*You* did it, Zack. You saved the world with ketchup."

"I helped to save the world, too, you know," said Zack's butt. "I did the hokeypokey."

"Yes." Eleanor smiled. "Zack and you."

"Thanks, Eleanor," said Zack, "but I think the real credit has to go to the mutant maggots. I mean, they had to *eat* the zombie butts."

"Yes, that's true," said the Forker. "But if I hadn't had the idea of doing the dance, then you couldn't have led the zombie butts to the Maggotorium and the maggots wouldn't have been able to eat them."

"If anyone deserves credit," said the Prince, "it's our master, the Mutant Maggot Lord. Without him, none of this would have been possible, would it, Maurice?"

"No, Your Highness," said Maurice, putting a butt-trumpet to his mouth and blowing a long impressive note. "And hail the Mutant Maggot Lord!"

The Mutant Maggot Lord dragged himself forward.

"Thank you," he said. "But the feast is not over yet."

Zack's stomach dropped as he tried to make sense of the Mutant Maggot Lord's words. "You mean . . ."

"Yes," said the Mutant Maggot Lord in a cold voice. "That's exactly what I mean."

"Well, well," said Eleanor, shaking her head in disgust. "What a surprise! Still the same old dirty double-crossing Kisser."

"You are a clever girl," said the Mutant Maggot Lord. "But perhaps not quite as clever as you think. Don't blame yourself, though. After all, I am a *very* charming man."

"Wrong," said Eleanor. "You *were* a very charming man. Now you're nothing but a sad mutant in a filthy sack."

"Maybe," said the Mutant Maggot Lord, "but soon you will be nothing but a munched-up morsel in a mutant maggot's belly. I, on the other hand, will rule the world."

"And just how do you propose to do that?" guffawed the Forker.

"With my mutant maggot army, of course," said the Mutant Maggot Lord. "The zombie butts were an unexpected interruption to my plans, but now that you have helped me to eliminate them, there is nothing to stop us! Nothing!"

"Except for the fact that your mutant maggots are too helpless to leave the Maggotorium," the Flicker said.

"They won't be mutant maggots for much longer," said the Mutant Maggot Lord. "Thanks to the nutritious feast you have just provided, they will soon be giant mutant blowflies. Squadrons of them — all under my command. But first, a little farewell supper."

"Aren't you forgetting something?" said Eleanor. "We're alive, and your mutant maggots don't eat *live* flesh.

"That can easily be remedied!" said the Mutant Maggot Lord.

As the Mutant Maggot Lord spoke, however, Zack began to notice through the gloom that the mutant maggots behind the Mutant Maggot Lord were not well.

They were twisting.

Writhing.

Convulsing.

Dying.

"I don't think your maggots will be eating anybody," said Zack.

"What are you talking about?" said the Mutant Maggot Lord.

"Turn around and see for yourself," said Zack.

The Mutant Maggot Lord dragged himself around.

"NO!" he cried. "NO!!!"

As the Mutant Maggot Lord pulled himself into their midst, the mutant maggots that were still alive threw themselves at him, temporarily blocking him from view. When they finally settled, Zack saw the Mutant Maggot Lord was sitting in the middle of the dying maggots, cradling one of them in his violently deformed arms. Well, at least Zack *thought* it was the Mutant Maggot Lord. His shroud had fallen from his head. Well, at least Zack *thought* it was his head. It seemed more like a blob of molten plastic, featureless except for a single sagging eye and a drooping mouth. Well, at least, Zack *thought* it was an eye and a mouth . . .

Zack stared at the figure.

"It's horrible," said Eleanor, grasping Zack's arm. "What is it?"

"It's the Mutant Maggot Lord's head," said Zack, finding his voice. "Well, at least I *think* it's the Mutant Maggot Lord's head . . ."

They watched as the Mutant Maggot Lord stroked the dead maggots.

And wept. Great heaving sobs.

Zack felt tears come into his own eyes. It was hard not to be moved by his grief.

Before long, all of the mutant maggots stopped moving. Zack, overcoming his revulsion, approached the Mutant Maggot Lord.

"It's over," said Zack. "There's nothing more you can do for them."

"I can at least be with them!" said the Mutant Maggot Lord.

"But they're dead," said Zack.

"And it's all my fault!" said the Mutant Maggot Lord.

"No, it was the zombie butts," said Zack, reaching out toward the Mutant Maggot Lord. "*They* killed your maggots."

"But my mutant maggots trusted me!" said the Mutant Maggot Lord, pushing Zack's hand away. "My beautiful babies trusted me and I led them to their doom."

"*Fed* them to their doom, you mean," said Zack's butt. Zack nudged it. "Shush," he said.

"We trusted you, too," said Eleanor. "But you were prepared to do the same to us."

The Mutant Maggot Lord looked at Eleanor with tears streaming from his eye.

"You are right," he whispered. "I am beneath contempt. I can hardly expect you to believe me when I say I am sorry, but I am. I truly am. For everything."

Zack could tell by Eleanor's silence that this time she did believe him.

"Come on," said Zack, stepping forward to pick up the Mutant Maggot Lord. "Come with us."

"Leave me!" said the Mutant Maggot Lord. "I need to be alone!"

Eleanor turned to Zack.

She nodded.

He shrugged. Zack realized there was nothing more they could do.

They turned and walked slowly through the dying maggots back toward the ladder where the Forker, the Flicker, and Gran were waiting.

Suddenly they heard a shout behind them.

"IT'S ALIVE!" cried the Mutant Maggot Lord.

Eleanor, Zack, and his butt turned to see an incredible sight. The Mutant Maggot Lord was excitedly hugging the maggot that only moments ago had been lying limp in his arms. "YOU'RE ALIVE!" he said, showering it with kisses. "YOU'RE ALIVE!"

But as they watched the Mutant Maggot Lord happily cradling the revived mutant maggot, Zack noticed another mutant maggot rise up behind him.

"Watch out!" yelled Zack.

But it was too late.

Before the Mutant Maggot Lord realized what was happening, the mutant maggot had struck. It had bitten his arm clean off. Well, at least Zack *thought* it was his arm . . .

Zack couldn't believe what he'd just seen.

Mutant maggots weren't supposed to eat living flesh.

Something was wrong.

Very wrong.

Something was as very wrong as it was possible for something very wrong to be.

"Behave yourself!" said the Mutant Maggot Lord, chiding his mutant maggots as if they'd simply scratched him. "Don't you remember who I am? I am your master! You love me! And I love you!"

But even as the Mutant Maggot Lord spoke, Zack saw the mutant maggot that he was cradling lift its ugly white head and remove his remaining arm — well, at least Zack *thought* it was his remaining arm — with a sickening crunch.

"Can we go home now?" said Zack's butt, as all the mutant maggots began to come alive. "I don't think I like this game anymore!"

"Best idea I've heard all day," said Gran.

"Don't be silly!" said the Mutant Maggot Lord. "There's nothing to be afraid of. They're my babies!"

"Not anymore they're not," said Eleanor, "They've been zombie-buttified . . . from the inside!"

"Oh no!" said the Flicker. "Not zombie mutant maggots!"

"Not exactly," said Eleanor. "I believe the technical term is 'mutant zombie maggots'!"

"Oh no!" said the Forker. "Not mutant zombie maggots!"

"Yes," said Eleanor. "Exactly!"

"No," said the Mutant Zombie Maggot Lord. "You've got it all wrong. They're just agitated."

"Gee," said Zack, narrowly dodging the slavering jaws of a mutant zombie maggot. "I'd hate to see them when they're *really* upset!"

"We're getting out of here," said Eleanor as the mutant zombie maggots began to close in around them. "Come on."

"What about me?" said the Mutant Zombie Maggot Lord.

"What about you?" said Eleanor. "You're a coward and a murderer. Find your own way out."

"But I haven't got any legs!" said the Mutant Zombie Maggot Lord. "Or arms!"

"Why don't you get the Prince and Maurice to help you?" said Eleanor. "Or have your little friends abandoned you?"

Zack looked around. He couldn't see them anywhere. The Mutant Zombie Maggot Lord was silent.

"Eleanor," said Zack, "we have to help him. He might be a Mutant Zombie Maggot Lord, but he's still a human being — or at least, he was."

"That's a matter of opinion," said Eleanor, delivering a double-handed powersmack to a mutant zombie maggot that was getting too close to her.

"Well, I'm going back for him," said Zack.

"No, Zack!" said his butt.

"I have to," said Zack.

Zack smacked and kicked his way through the gradually reviving mutant zombie maggots back to where the Mutant Zombie Maggot Lord — or what remained of him — was lying in a pool of blood, shivering.

Zack picked him up and slung him over his shoulder. He couldn't believe how light he was.

Zack turned to leave, but at that moment a particularly large and ugly mutant zombie maggot blocked his path.

Zack tried to kick it.

Zack tried to smack it.

Zack tried to pinch it.

He even tried the hokeypokey.

But nothing worked.

Not only had the mutant zombie maggots acquired the zombie butts' resistance to pain, but having no arms or legs gave them natural immunity to the power of the hokeypokey as well.

The mutant zombie maggot opened its mouth wide.

Zack looked up to see an enormous black cavern above him.

He closed his eyes. This was going to be worse than any death he had experienced in the butt-fighting simulator.

Well, there were perhaps worse deaths, but this one was real.

Suddenly there was a sharp crack, followed by a massive explosion.

Zack opened his eyes. The Flicker was standing a few yards behind where the mutant zombie maggot had been, towel in hand.

"Gotcha!" said the Flicker.

The Flicker had flicked the zombie mutant maggot so hard it had exploded. Zack looked at the pieces around him . . . and then yelled as he watched them slowly slide toward one another.

At that moment, Zack realized the terrible truth: The mutant zombie maggots were completely indestructible!

"Well, don't just stand there!" said the Flicker, forging

a gristly path through the mutant zombie maggots with a blitzkrieg of brutal towel flicking. "Follow me!"

As he picked his way carefully through the trail of mutant zombie maggot meat that led to the ladder, Zack could hear the Mutant Zombie Maggot Lord whimpering.

But although they were moving fast, the increasingly manic mutant zombie maggots were faster. They surged ahead of the Flicker and Zack and clumped together around the foot of the ladder, forming a formidable barrier that was proving practically impossible for the Flicker to crack open.

The Flicker flicked his towel against the wall of maggots to no avail.

"Can we get through?" said Zack.

"Not this way!" said the Flicker as the mutant zombie maggots closed in around them. "There's too many. I flick one and another takes its place. We're going to have to try and jump across them."

Zack gulped. He wished he had his butt with him.

It was a big jump. A huge jump. An enormous jump.

And failure would mean landing right in the middle of the mutant zombie maggot clump.

Even without the Mutant Zombie Maggot Lord in his arms, it would have been a big call. But it wasn't like he had another way out of the Maggotorium.

"Come on, Zack," said the Flicker. "You first."

Zack took a deep breath. He was about to jump when the Mutant Zombie Maggot Lord spoke. "No!" he said. "Put me down. I'll lure them away from the ladder while you both escape."

"No way," said Zack. "They'll eat you alive."

"No they won't," said the Mutant Zombie Maggot Lord. "They're *good* boys and girls really . . . I can't understand what's got into them!"

"Zombie butts got into them!" said the Flicker. "That's what!"

"Go," said the Mutant Zombie Maggot Lord. "Please, it will be better if I'm alone. They've never taken to strangers very well."

Zack shook his head. "They're out of control!" he said. "They'll kill you!"

"I think I can settle them," insisted the Mutant Zombie Maggot Lord.

Zack stared into the Mutant Zombie Maggot Lord's eye — at least he thought it was an eye. "If that's what you want," he said.

"That's what I want," said the Mutant Zombie Maggot Lord.

Zack laid the Mutant Maggot Lord on the ground as he had requested. The clump of mutant zombie maggots surged toward him.

"Thank you," said the Mutant Zombie Maggot Lord. The mutant zombie maggots slithered around him. "Now go . . . your friends are waiting . . . and so are mine."

Zack nodded. He and the Flicker stepped gingerly across the ground to the ladder and started climbing.

As fast as they could.

The butt-fighters were about halfway up the ladder when the Maggotorium was filled with a bloodcurdling scream.

They stopped climbing and looked at one onother.

Nobody spoke a word.

Nobody needed to.

It was clear that they all knew exactly what the scream meant.

The Mutant Zombie Maggot Lord was dead.

"I never liked him," said the Forker, breaking the silence. "It just goes to prove the old butt-fighter's proverb."

"Which one?" said the Flicker.

"He who lives by the maggot, dies by the maggot," said the Forker, solemnly.

"I've never heard that proverb," said the Flicker.

"No," said the Forker, "you wouldn't have, because I just made it up."

"Then how can it be an *old* butt-fighter's proverb?"

"Because I'm an *old* butt-fighter!" said the Forker.

"Will you two quit joking around!" said Eleanor. "This is SERIOUS!"

"Oh, I don't know," said the Flicker. "I don't like mutant zombie maggots any more than you do, but it's not as if they can climb the ladder, is it?"

"They don't need to," said Eleanor, pointing down. "Look!"

Zack looked down and through the gloom saw that the mutant zombie maggots were clumping together in what appeared to be a massive game of Jenga. They were entwining themselves around and on top of one another, and forming a white tower of mutant zombie maggots that was rising rapidly toward them.

"Oh, no!" said Zack's butt. "A mutant zombie maggot *tower*!"

The Flicker screwed his face up and stroked his chin. "Actually," he said, "on second thought, this *is* serious."

"Quick!" said Eleanor. "We have to get to the top and seal off the entrance before the giant zombie mutant maggots can escape!"

The butt-fighters didn't need any encouragement.

They climbed as fast as they possibly could.

But the mutant zombie maggot tower was faster.

●● ●● ●●

By the time Zack reached the top of the ladder, the putrid pile of mutant zombie maggots was only a few yards below him.

"Quick, Zack!" yelled his butt, reaching over the edge to help Zack out.

"Thanks!" said Zack as his butt dragged him clear. He was about to stand up when a mutant zombie maggot leaped out after him. It landed on top of Zack, pinning him to the ground.

"Ugh!" said Zack, struggling to breathe underneath the massive mutant zombie maggot's weight. "Help!"

Fortunately for Zack, however, Mabel's Angels were right beside him. They snapped into action like a lethal, well-oiled butt-fighting machine.

Unfortunately for Zack, however, Mabel's Angels were

unable to land a single fork, pinch, or towel flick before the mutant zombie maggot raised its ugly head in the air and repelled them with its disgusting gale-force mutant zombie maggot breath.

Zack watched them tumble backward into a helpless heap on the ground.

"Well," said Zack's butt. "That seemed to go well. I guess that's it then."

"Not quite," said Eleanor, pointing her Laxative Launcher at the mutant zombie maggot. "Sweet dreams."

The mutant zombie maggot roared again and lunged at Eleanor. She stepped backward and emptied the contents of the 4502-LL into its mouth and started counting. "One . . . two . . . three!"

The laxative capsules had a dramatic effect. Under the force of its own violently expelled waste, the mutant zombie maggot took off into the air in a series of helter-skelter zigs, zags, and loops. It was not unlike what happens when a balloon is blown up and then let free without tying its neck. Not a pretty sight by any definition of the term *pretty sight*, but extremely effective.

Zack drew a deep breath. "Thanks," he said, getting to his knees and wiping mutant zombie maggot mush out of his eyes. "I owe you one."

"If we live long enough," said Eleanor.

"What do you mean?" said Zack.

"Um, Zack," said his butt. "I don't know if you've noticed, but we're surrounded."

Zack turned to see a great white stream of mutant

zombie maggots spewing from the Maggotorium entrance. The delay had cost them dearly. The mutant zombie maggots had encircled them, completely cutting them off from the butt-mobile.

"What are we going to do, Eleanor?" said Zack.

"I give up," said Eleanor. "I'm a butt-fighter, not a mutant zombie maggot fighter. And I'm all out of laxative capsules."

"But we can't just give up!" said Zack. "The whole of Mabeltown — no, the whole PLANET — is relying on us! If these mutant zombie maggots break free, then the whole world is doomed!"

"They already have broken free, Zack," said Eleanor quietly. "Don't you get it? It's over. We tried. We failed."

"No way!" said Zack.

"You're exactly right," said Eleanor. "There is no way."

"No," said Zack. "I meant no way is there no way!"

"No way is there no way that there is no way," said Eleanor.

Suddenly a brilliant light shot across the sky.

A light so white and so bright that they had to shield their eyes from the painful glare.

Nobody had any idea what it was.

Nobody, that is, except for Zack Freeman.

He remembered the buttmergency transmitter button he'd pushed back in Silas Sterne's office. His message must have gotten through.

New hope surged into his body.

His parents had returned from Uranus! They would know what to do.

Gran and her angels were a little past their use-by dates when it came to modern butt-fighting. But his parents were two of the top interplanetary butt-fighters in the world. They would know *exactly* how to handle the situation.

Zack was sure of it. "Way," he said quietly.

CHAPTER THIRTEEN

Many Crappy Returns

The fiery object blazed down out of the sky and crashed into the middle of the park. A deafening sonic boom followed close behind, splitting the air — and everybody's eardrums — with a thunderous crack. Zack could feel the vibrations deep in his chest.

"What a crack!" said the Flicker.

"Language!" said Gran.

"I meant the sound," said the Flicker.

"Oh, that's all right then," said Gran. "I thought you meant —"

"Phwoar!" said the Forker. "What's that smell?"

"I don't know," said Eleanor. "But whatever it is, it's the first nice thing I've smelled all day."

Zack sniffed deeply.

He knew that smell.

It was his mother's perfume!

He closed his eyes and took another deep breath. It

had been a long time since he had smelled anything so good. In fact, it had been a long time since he'd smelled anything good at all.

"Look, Zack!" said his butt, tugging on his hand. "The mutant zombie maggots! They're scared!"

Zack opened his eyes and saw that the mutant zombie maggots that had been closing in on them only moments before were now fleeing toward the edge of the park, clearly repelled. "Perhaps they don't like the smell," said Zack.

Zack had to hand it to his parents. It was a brilliant strategy.

"What do you think it is?" said Gran.

"I don't know," said the Forker, "but whatever it is, I think it's on our side."

"I *know* it's on our side," said Zack, beaming.

"How can you be so sure?" said Eleanor.

"Remember the message I sent to my parents back at the Academy?" said Zack. "I wasn't sure whether they'd even get it, but here they are . . . just in time! They've been to Uranus. They'll know what to do."

Gran nodded her approval. "Good work, soldier," she said.

Eleanor shrugged. "My father went to Uranus, too," she said. "But it didn't stop him from being zombie-buttified."

As Zack strained to catch a glimpse of his parents' butt-mobile through the blinding haze he considered Eleanor's point.

What if she was right?

What if his parents *didn't* know what to do?

What if they had already been zombie-buttified on Uranus and had returned not to save the world, but to help destroy it?

Zack watched as the light became brighter and brighter, until finally the smoke cleared and the true cause of the incredible luminescence emerged.

Zack drew in his breath sharply.

It wasn't his parents.

It wasn't even his zombie-buttified parents.

It was worse.

It was the Great White Butt!

●● ●● ●●

Zack was stunned.

It *couldn't* be the Great White Butt.

It certainly didn't *smell* like the Great White Butt.

"I thought you said the Great White Butt was dead," said Gran, frowning. "It doesn't look too dead to me."

"It *was* dead!" said Zack. "I scored a direct hit with a butt-harpoon and then buttcano-blasted it into outer space!"

"It's true," said Eleanor. "I saw it."

"Yes," said the Forker. "But did he *kill* it?"

"I *thought* I killed it," said Zack. "Well, as good as, anyway."

"Not good enough, apparently," said the Flicker.

"No," said Zack. "I guess the Kicker was right about me after all. I can't even kill a butt-eyed buttcano-blasted butt!"

At that moment the enormous butt guffawed, assailing the butt-fighters with the nauseating odor of its breath.

Zack gagged.

There was no mistaking that stale nostril-scorching stench.

It was the Great White Butt all right.

"Don't feel so bad, Zack," said the enormous butt. "You just forgot who you were dealing with. I AM the Great White Butt after all . . . indestructible AND immortal."

"Oh, Master!" said a voice from behind Zack. "Oh Great and Glorious White Butt from the sky, you are very welcome!"

"Yes," echoed Maurice. "Very, *very* welcome!"

Zack turned to see the Prince and Maurice bowing and scraping the ground in front of them as they approached.

"Where are the zombie butts?" bellowed the Great White Butt.

"They have all been eaten by the mutant maggots," said the Prince, pointing to the writhing masses around the park's edge. "The planet is safe and ready for you to take over, thanks to us, your humble and faithful servants."

The Great White Butt glowed white with rage.

"FOOLS!" it said, picking them both up by their legs, clonking them hard together and then hurling their limp bodies across the park toward the mutant zombie maggots. There was a brief frenzy among the mutant zombie maggots and the Prince and Maurice disappeared.

Zack shuddered. Although he had no great affection

for either of them, he didn't think they deserved a fate like that. The Prince and Maurice were just a couple of harmless buffoons. On the other hand, the Great White Butt was an evil mastermind intent on total buttimation of the univarse. He really *did* deserve it.

"Well, Zack," said the Great White Butt, turning its attention back to him. "It *is* a small univarse, isn't it! You know, I was just talking to your parents about you . . ."

"Yeah, right," said Zack.

"No, it's true," said the Great White Butt. "I met them on Uranus."

"Language!" said Gran.

"I meant the planet!" said the Great White Butt.

"It's not possible," said Zack.

"Of course I meant the planet," said the Great White Butt. "What else could I have meant?"

"I'm not talking about that," said Zack. "I mean it's not possible that you could have met my parents on Uranus."

"Language!" said Gran.

"I meant the planet," said Zack.

"Oh yes," said the Great White Butt. "After you blew me out of the buttcano, I was in a bad way. I flew through space, bleeding, on fire, missing the skin from one cheek and landed on Uranus."

"Language!" said Gran.

"I meant the planet," said the Great White Butt. "Well, what's left of it. You see, there was a lot of methane and I was on fire and there was a rather large — and smelly — explosion."

"So that's how the zombie butts reanimated and became zombies!" said Eleanor.

"Yes," continued the Great White Butt. "Unfortunately I ended up stuck down a very deep hole. But your parents, Zack, were kind enough to wake me up. And then your mother went and spoiled her good deed by throwing a perfume bomb at me. They were such a nice couple. It was almost a shame I had to kill them."

"You what?" said Zack, shocked.

"You heard," said the Great White Butt. "It was nothing personal, you understand. Purely business. YOU — on the other hand — you I will kill for pleasure."

"Not if I can help it," said Gran.

"Silence, you ridiculous old hag!" shouted the Great White Butt, turning its attention to her. "Don't I know you from somewhere?"

"Unfortunately, yes," said Gran. "Siberia, remember? We tarred and feathered you and ran you out of town."

"Oh yes," said the Great White Butt. "I remember. I still bear the scars. It wasn't very friendly of you."

"I'm not a very friendly old woman," Gran said. "Now prepare to die!"

"Why?" said the Great White Butt. "Who's going to kill me?"

"Me!" said Gran.

"Oh really?" said the Great White Butt. "You and whose army?"

Gran stepped forward. "My army," she said. "Mabel's Angels!"

The Forker and the Flicker stepped up next to her, and

all three of them snapped into action like a lethal, well-oiled butt-fighting machine.

Unfortunately, however, Mabel's Angels were unable to land a single fork, pinch, or towel-flick before the Great White Butt blasted three deadly accurate bursts of gas at them. The butt-fighters fell to the ground in an unconscious heap.

Eleanor shook her head.

"Well," said Zack's butt. "I'm certainly glad they're here — otherwise we'd be in *real* trouble."

Zack looked at Gran — and her Angels — helpless on the ground beside the Great White Butt's crater. He couldn't tell if they were dead or just gassed, but they weren't moving and their tongues were hanging out of their mouths. It didn't look good.

Zack looked at the Great White Butt.

He felt himself trembling with anger.

He couldn't hold back any longer.

It was time to act.

Time to finish the job he'd started back in the buttcano.

But he'd have to be careful.

The Great White Butt was strong.

Zack knew that.

He was also painfully aware that every time he tried to do something he usually ended up making the situation worse than if he'd done nothing at all. In fact, he was beginning to think that the most effective and powerful course of action he could possibly take was exactly that: to do nothing at all.

So, unable to hold back any longer, he did exactly that.

Nothing.

At all.

Eleanor, however, had other ideas.

"Murderer!" she screamed, and flew through the air in the classic double-footed, double-handed kick-slap attack position.

"Butt-hater!" said the Great White Butt, slapping her to the ground.

Zack watched, terrified, as the Great White Butt climbed out of the crater and lumbered toward the four limp bodies.

"I'm so tired," said the Great White Butt, yawning and lowering itself down over the top of them all. "And it's been such a long trip. I think I'll have a little rest!"

Zack gasped.

He realized that his decision to do nothing at all couldn't possibly be any worse than doing something. Anything!

"No!" he yelled, getting to his feet and charging forward.

"Zack!" yelled his butt. "Don't do anything stupid."

But it was too late.

Zack stood directly in front of the Great White Butt. "Get away from them," he demanded.

"Mind your own business," said the Great White Butt.

"They are my business," said Zack. "And so are you. I killed you once and I'll kill you again!"

"Correction!" said the Great White Butt. "You *almost*

killed me once. And that was with the help of a butt-harpoon. What are you going to do without that? Bore me to death?"

Zack stopped and thought.

Or at least he *tried* to think.

The smell of his mother's perfume bomb was overwhelming and made it very difficult to think about anything at all.

Then Zack remembered.

He had something greater than Silas Sterne's butt-harpoon. And something even more powerful than his mother's perfume.

Ketchup!

He took the bottle from his belt, knelt down, and pointed it at the Great White Butt. The perfume bomb would be no protection against the mutant zombie maggots once Zack had neutralized the perfume with ketchup. The Great White Butt was about to become mutant zombie maggot food.

And by the way it had begun to tremble, Zack could see that the Great White Butt knew it, too.

"I wouldn't do that if I were you," it said.

"And why not?" asked Zack.

"Because the moment you squirt me," said the Great White Butt, "not only will I lose the protection of your mother's perfume bomb, but so will you."

Even though Zack was no stranger to sacrificing his life, he hesitated. He'd almost died once before and he hadn't much enjoyed the experience. His mind flashed back to the buttcano. The death stink. The match. The gas. The explosion . . .

"What are you waiting for, Zack?" yelled Eleanor, who had revived sufficiently to be aware of what was happening. "Squirt!"

"Don't be a fool!" said the Great White Butt.

Zack thought hard. Well, as hard as it was possible to think when you could hardly think. In fact, he didn't think at all. He remembered.

His mother.

His father.

His gran.

The Forker.

The Flicker.

Eleanor's mother.

Eleanor's father.

The Smacker.

The Kicker.

The Kisser.

The Prince and Maurice.

Even Uranus (the planet).

How many more had to die?

When would the squashings and gassings and "rather large explosions" stop?

Zack tightened his grip of the squeeze bottle.

He might have failed to save the world from the mutant zombie maggots, but he could at least save the world, once and for all, from the threat of the Great White Butt.

He closed his eyes and pressed hard on the squeeze bottle.

But nothing happened.

He pressed it again.

This time the bottle made a farty sound.

Empty!

Zack realized with a shock that he'd used every last drop of ketchup on preparing the zombie butts for the mutant maggot feast.

The Great White Butt laughed.

Zack was now completely helpless.

"Time to die, boy," hissed the Great White Butt.

●● ●● ●●

"Over my dead body!" yelled Gran.

"What are you doing still alive?" said the Great White Butt, clearly surprised. "I thought I gassed you!"

Gran smiled. "When you've breathed as much methane as I have," she said, "a little bit more doesn't make a whole lot of difference."

She circled the Great White Butt as she spoke, her fingers in pincer formation, snapping menacingly at its thin white legs.

The Great White Butt laughed, emitting great gusts of methane.

Gran, however, continued undaunted. She managed to land a pinch on the Great White Butt's left knee.

"Go, Gran!" yelled Zack's butt.

The Great White Butt howled and jerked its leg out involuntarily, sending Gran flying into the middle of the mutant zombie maggots.

Zack drew his breath in sharply.

His gran was surrounded by mutant zombie maggots, all about to strike.

He could hardly watch.

He'd already lost his parents.

He couldn't bear to lose his gran as well.

Not that he need have worried.

Gran stood up, looked around her, and then did an extraordinary thing.

She started to spin around on the spot — snipping and snapping the air with her pincer-fingers.

Within moments, all the mutant zombie maggots around her had lost their heads. Then, before they had a chance to repair themselves, Gran spun herself forward, cutting a deadly slash through the hapless and increasingly headless sea of maggots back toward the Great White Butt. She was like a one-woman tornado, extracting maximum damage on the mutant zombie maggots.

Eleanor shook her head in admiration. "Awesome," she said.

"Not bad," said Zack's butt. "Not bad at all."

Zack nodded. "That's my gran," he said proudly.

But just as Gran was about to reach them, a mutant zombie maggot dodged her pincers, grabbed her around the waist, and started pulling her back into the frenzied mass. Gran tried digging her fingers into the ground in front of her, but it was no use. The mutant zombie maggot was too strong.

"Aawww," said the Great White Butt with mock disappointment. "Just when she was doing so well, too."

Suddenly there was a loud whoosh, and Zack saw a flash of silver fly through the air. A large fork had embedded itself in the mutant zombie maggot's flesh. The mutant zombie maggot spun around. Gran jumped free and ran across the park at the Great White Butt with a bloodcurdling scream.

"Calm down!" said the Great White Butt, emitting great gusts of wind, which Zack assumed was laughter. As Gran got close, it reached down and grabbed her in its rubbery hand. "You'll give yourself a heart attack carrying on like that!"

"Put her down!" boomed the Forker.

Zack looked at the Forker and the Flicker. They were fully revived and about to unload a double-pronged blitzkrieg of fork and towel-flick power on the Great White Butt.

"Don't worry about me," shouted Gran. "I'll handle this oaf. Save yourselves! That's an order!"

"That's an order we cannot obey!" said the Forker, his hands no more than a blur as he assembled the biggest fork that Zack had ever seen. It was twice as big as the Forker himself, with prongs as long and wide as fence pickets. "Stand by for MEGA-FORK launch! Count me down, Flicker!"

The Flicker smiled broadly. "Five, four, three, two, one!" he said, cracking his towel. The Forker hurled the mighty fork.

Zack saw the Great White Butt flinch as the four deadly prongs of the mega-fork surged through the air toward it.

But the Great White Butt was too fast. It emitted a powerful blast of gas that turned the mega-fork around in mid-flight and sent it hurtling back toward the Forker and the Flicker.

"It's coming back!" cried the Flicker.

"Well don't just stand there," said the Forker. "RUN, you idiot!"

"You're the idiot!" said the Flicker. "It's your mega-fork!"

"Language!" said Gran, struggling to escape the Great White Butt's grip.

The Forker and the Flicker turned to run, but the mega-fork was traveling too fast. It plunged deep into the ground, trapping them both between its enormous prongs.

"Mega-fork!" said the Flicker, shaking his head. "What a stupid idea!"

"It's never failed before," said the Forker.

"Have you ever actually *used* it before?" said the Flicker.

"No," said the Forker.

Zack looked around him.

As usual, the situation was not good.

The Great White Butt was holding Gran prisoner.

The Forker and the Flicker were trapped underneath a giant fork.

Eleanor was out of laxative capsules and Zack was out of ketchup.

Oh, and they were surrounded by indestructible mutant zombie maggots.

Not a good situation no matter how you looked at it.

"Put me down right now, you fat lump of rancid lard!" said Gran, still struggling, "or you'll be sorry!"

"Language, Pincher!" said the Great White Butt, chuckling again. "The only thing I'm going to be sorry about is that none of you will be alive to see the course of buttolution reach its natural conclusion! Once the mutant zombie maggots have done their work and eliminated all human resistance, they'll simply consume themselves and then the Earth will be mine. ALL mine."

"And then what?" said Eleanor. "What in the univarse could possibly be the point of owning an empty, devastated planet?"

"Ahh," said the Great White Butt. "You have so little imagination! But that's understandable; after all, it is your head talking and not your butt. Can't you see? It's not the Earth that I want. It's the entire univarse! But I have to start somewhere. The Earth is not much, but it will do."

As the Great White Butt blathered on about his plans for the total buttification of the univarse, Zack noticed that Gran had passed out again. It didn't surprise him. He wasn't feeling too great himself. The combination of the Great White Butt's breath, incredible brightness, intense heat, and overpowering perfume-bomb stench all combined to make him feel extremely light-headed and dizzy.

"We're doomed, Zack!" whispered his butt. "We're doomed and we're going to die."

Zack blinked as he surveyed the hopeless scene in front of him.

It was hard not to agree.

All of the mutant zombie maggots injured by Gran appeared to have restored themselves. In fact, they looked more formidable than before. Some even had dangerous-looking black bristles sprouting out from their smooth white skins.

Hang on, thought Zack. Black bristles?

He wondered if he was starting to hallucinate.

"Hey!" he said in a low voice to Eleanor. "Do those maggots have bristles or am I seeing things?"

Eleanor looked at the maggots and then nodded.

"Yes," she said. "They do! But mutant zombie maggots don't have black bristles . . . not unless . . ." She gripped Zack's arm. "Do you think they're about to change into blowflies?"

"Well," said Zack, "it's certainly possible. The Mutant Zombie Maggot Lord said they would."

"Oh no," said his butt. "Not giant mutant zombie blowflies! That's terrible!"

"Don't panic," said Zack. "Remember the giant blowflies that chased us in the Sea of Butts? It wasn't us they wanted — it was the poopoises, because of what they were made of. And there's no poopoises around here, so we should be perfectly safe. But I sure am glad I'm not the Great White Butt."

Eleanor smiled and nodded. "This should be good," she said.

The mutant zombie maggots were changing fast now.

The heat and light generated by the Great White Butt's enthusiasm for itself and its deluded quest had provided the perfect conditions for supercharging the mutant zombie maggot metabolism.

They all had bristles.

Most were growing legs and wings.

A few were even sprouting the giant proboscises that Zack remembered only too well.

The sound of frantic buzzing filled the air as the giant

mutant zombie blowflies tested out their new wings. Before the Great White Butt had stopped talking and realized what was happening, they rose in a thick black swarm all around it.

Zack, Eleanor, and Zack's butt turned and high-fived one another.

But the giant mutant zombie blowflies didn't attack the Great White Butt.

They couldn't attack it.

The giant zombie mutant blowflies began to fly away, clearly as repulsed by the perfume as they had been when they were mutant zombie maggots.

The Great White Butt laughed. "This really must be my lucky day!" it said. "And it's not my birthday till next week!"

Zack and Eleanor and his butt looked at one another in utter despair.

The giant mutant zombie blowflies would now fly away and breed, producing ever-increasing amounts of new mutant zombie maggots that would spread all over the planet in a matter of weeks.

And the Great White Butt was still alive.

A tear rolled down Zack's cheek.

He wasn't going to save the world after all.

He couldn't even save himself.

"Don't cry," said his butt gently.

"Why not?" said Zack.

"Because I have a plan!" it whispered.

"What could you possibly do that we haven't already tried?" said Eleanor.

"Watch this!" said his butt. It detached itself from

Zack's body and floated up in front of the Great White Butt.

"What do you want?" said the Great White Butt.

"Did I hear you say it was your birthday next week?" said Zack's butt.

"Yes," said the Great White Butt. "Next Wednesday. Why?"

"Well, in that case," said Zack's butt, "please allow me to give you an early birthday present!"

"It's not necessary," said the Great White Butt. "I already have all I desire."

"But not all you deserve," said Zack's butt.

"What are you talking about?" said the Great White Butt.

Zack's butt's only reply was to bend over, summon all of its energy, and blast its deadly payload all over the Great White Butt.

"Many crappy returns of the day!" it said.

CHAPTER FOURTEEN

The Brown Hole

Zack's butt's early birthday present instantly neutralized the effects of the perfume bomb.

The result was as swift as it was dramatic.

The Great White Butt's natural odor blasted through the air like a sonic boom — only there was no sound — just a sickening wave of stink.

Zack watched as the giant mutant zombie blowflies picked up the scent, circled around, and returned in a thick swarm. "Quick," said Zack to his butt. "Hide before they smell you as well!"

Zack's butt made a beeline for Zack's pants.

"Get us out of here!" said the Flicker, still trapped under the prongs of the mega-fork with the Forker.

Zack and Eleanor ran across and tried to lift the fork out of the ground. But it was no use. The mega-fork was in too deep. And within moments the air around them was filled with giant mutant zombie blowflies. They ran to take cover in the drain. "We'll be back," called Eleanor.

The giant mutant zombie blowflies were attacking the Great White Butt from all angles, bombarding him with the yellowish-green gunk they used to help soften and partially digest their food before eating it.

"Blast you, you infernal giant mutant zombie blowflies!" yelled the Great White Butt, as it danced around using Gran as a flyswatter. "And blast you, Zack Freeman, AND your meddling butt!"

"Language!" yelled Gran as she went whizzing through the gunk-filled air, occasionally colliding with a giant mutant zombie blowfly.

But the Great White Butt was fighting a losing battle. Without its perfume shield the enormous butt was helpless against the relentless onslaught of the giant mutant zombie blowflies.

Finally it did the only thing it could do.

The Great White Butt crouched down and blasted off from Earth with as much thrust as it could muster.

Zack watched as the Great White Butt soared into the air with the cloud of giant zombie mutant blowflies in hot pursuit.

"Gran!" yelled Zack. "We have to save her!"

"Are you crazy?" said his butt.

"No," said Zack, climbing out of the drain. He ran to a giant mutant zombie blowfly that had been stunned in the attack. "I'd do the same for you." He quickly un-rolled some toilet paper from his belt and lassoed it around the giant mutant zombie blowfly's neck. Then, grabbing hold of one of its bristles, he swung himself up onto the giant mutant zombie blowfly's back.

"I'm coming with you!" said Eleanor, swinging herself up behind Zack. "It's payback time." She sat behind him and put her arms around his waist.

"Good luck!" yelled the Forker.

"We'll just wait here!" yelled the Flicker.

Zack and Eleanor waved.

"I hope you know what you're doing!" said Zack's butt.

"Me, too!" said Zack, converting the lasso into a set of makeshift reins and flicking them hard against the giant mutant zombie blowfly's throbbing thorax. With a start, it jumped up into the air and joined in the pursuit of the Great White Butt.

"Where did you learn to ride giant mutant zombie blowflies?" said Eleanor.

"In the butt-fighting simulator," said Zack. "It was one of the few things I wasn't completely crap at."

"Language!" yelled Gran from up ahead of them.

The Great White Butt zigzagged and looped and flew at tremendous speeds in an attempt to shake the giant mutant zombie blowflies, but nothing worked.

Zack managed to gain on the mob of blowflies and draw to the front. He reached over and, using the giant mutant zombie blowfly's proboscis like a fire hose, blasted the Great White Butt with goo.

"Watch out where you're pointing that thing!" said Gran, who seemed to be bearing the brunt of the goo attack.

Finally — unable to shake the giant mutant zombie blowflies — the Great White Butt zoomed straight up into the air, passed through the clouds, and just kept going.

Straight up.

"Uh-oh," said Eleanor, visibly shivering. "We're in trouble now."

"I thought we already were," said Zack, who was also starting to shiver.

"No, really big trouble," said Eleanor.

"I thought we were already in that as well," said Zack.

"No, really, really big trouble!" said Eleanor. "The Great White Butt can't lose the blowflies on Earth, so it's heading out into space!"

"That's brilliant!" said Zack. "The blowflies will follow it out there and before they realize where they are they'll be frozen to death! You've got to hand it to the Great White Butt. It's not stupid!"

"No," said Eleanor. "But YOU ARE!"

"Why do you say that?" said Zack.

"In case you hadn't noticed," said Zack's butt, "the Great White Butt has still got Gran around the neck. It's taking her with it."

"That's really bad," said Zack.

"It's more than really bad," said Eleanor. "It's REALLY, REALLY bad! We're heading into space with no protection whatsoever — not even a warm sweater! Don't you remember what Dad taught you about the danger of unprepared space travel during his lecture on interplanetary butt-fighting?"

The air was thinning and Zack was finding it difficult

to think. He vaguely remembered the lecture, but he had been very tired at the time and had nodded off once or twice. "Sort of," he said.

"Let me remind you," said Eleanor, quoting from memory. " 'Exposed to the vacuum of space, your body fluids would quickly boil. Bubbles would form in your blood vessels and body tissues, causing them to rupture. All the gases inside your body would expand. You would become unconscious in about fifteen seconds. You would have permanent brain damage in about four minutes. That's if your skin wasn't punctured by small, high-speed particles traveling through space. Or you weren't instantly snap-frozen in temperatures as low as minus one hundred degrees, or turned into galactic fried human in temperatures as high as three hundred degrees in the full glare of the sun.' "

"But what about Gran?" said Zack.

"What about us?" said Eleanor. "Maybe we have to let her go."

"No way!" said Zack.

"But it's not worth all of us dying, Zack!" said Eleanor, reaching for the reins. "We have to turn back!"

"Just a little bit longer!" said Zack, pulling the reins away from Eleanor's grasping hands. "If we can just go a little bit faster . . ."

"No!" said Eleanor, making a desperate lunge for control of the giant mutant zombie blowfly.

Zack jerked his hands upward.

Suddenly there was the sound of tearing toilet paper.

Zack stared at the shreds of the reins in his hands as

the now uncontrollable giant mutant zombie blowfly continued its pursuit of the Great White Butt into space.

"Now you've done it!" said Eleanor.

"I didn't do it," said Zack. "You did!"

"You BOTH did it!" said Zack's butt.

Zack and Eleanor glared at each other.

"Well, I guess this is it," said Zack, finally shrugging. "We can't survive in outer space without spacesuits."

He felt his butt shrug. "It's not impossible," it said.

"How could it not be impossible?" said Eleanor.

"We need a bubble shield," said his butt.

"A what?" said Zack.

"A bubble shield," said Zack's butt. "I can make one."

"I don't think so!" said Zack. He wasn't sure what a bubble shield was, exactly, but he didn't like the sound of it. Or the smell of it, for that matter.

"No way," said Eleanor.

Zack's butt sounded slightly hurt. "It's your choice," it said. "I just thought that you might both prefer NOT to have all the fluids in your body boil. I kind of had this silly idea that you might think it was better to AVOID having bubbles form in your blood vessels and body tissues that would cause them to rupture. And, call me crazy, but is having all the gases in your body expand, becoming unconscious in about fifteen seconds, having permanent brain damage after four minutes, and being subjected to temperatures as low as minus one hundred degrees and as high as three hundred degrees in the full glare of the sun REALLY the way you both hoped to die?"

"Well, now that you put it like that," said Zack, "maybe it is worth a try."

Eleanor nodded. "It won't be for long, anyhow. Once the Great White Butt has destroyed the giant mutant zombie blowflies, it will hightail it back into the atmosphere as fast it can."

"I knew you'd see it my way," said Zack's butt, beginning to emit enough gas to form a protective bubble that would cocoon itself, Zack, and Eleanor against the ravages of outer space.

As it did so, they rapidly passed through the upper layers of the atmosphere. They rocketed through a range of colors, the shades of which Zack had never seen before — extraordinary greens and reds and rich purples that gradually merged into the infinite blackness of space.

Zack marveled at its beauty, despite the pungency of the bubble shield.

He looked down.

Not only could he see the blue Earth curving away from him in all directions, but he saw the zombie blowflies still in hot pursuit.

Zack couldn't figure it out.

It wasn't possible.

Then it hit him.

It was obvious.

They weren't ordinary flies.

They were *zombie* flies.

Outer space couldn't kill them.

They were already dead.

It began to dawn on Zack that this might not be quite as short a trip into outer space as they had hoped.

The Great White Butt sped up. It was already going fast. Unencumbered by gravity it was traveling at more than one hundred times the speed of wind.

And now it was going faster still.

It passed the Moon.

It passed Mars.

"Where in the univarse is it going?" said Eleanor.

"I don't know," said Zack's butt. "But I sure hope we get there soon. I can't keep up this shield forever, you know."

And then, up ahead, they saw something more scary than zombie butts, mutant zombie maggots, and giant mutant zombie blowflies put together.

A huge swirling brown vortex.

A brown hole — the most destructive force in the univarse — and they were headed straight for it!

* * *

Zack stared at the brown hole.

It was terrifying.

He recalled the Blind Butt-feeler's words: *Fear not the brown hole.* At the time he'd thought it was a baffling piece of advice. And now that he was face-to-face with one, he was even more confused.

How was it possible *not* to fear a brown hole?

In his lecture on interplanetary butt-fighting, Silas Sterne had thumped the lectern as he tried to impress on the students just how dangerous a brown hole was. That not even the most experienced, most skilled butt-fighters stood a snowball's chance in hell of surviving a close encounter with one of these monsters. "Because, make no mistake," Silas had said, "that is what they are! Monsters! They'll suck you in, chew you up and then . . . well, if by some miracle you were lucky enough to make it out the other end, you can be sure of one thing: It wouldn't be the same place you went in. The forces inside a brown hole are so powerful that they warp the very fabric of space. You could find yourself crawling out into another solar system . . . another galaxy . . . maybe even a whole other univarse! One thing's for sure: The chances of making it back home again are a zillion to none. A brown hole is a one-way roller coaster into the unknown. AVOID THEM AT ALL COSTS!"

Zack was more than willing to avoid this particular brown hole at all costs, but it was a little difficult when the giant mutant zombie blowfly they were riding was hell-bent on pursuing the Great White Butt, and the Great White Butt was hell-bent on heading straight for the brown hole.

Zack could feel the hairs being sucked out of his scalp, his eyes being sucked out of their sockets, and — worst of all — his butt being sucked off his body.

"Help me, Zack!" yelled his butt. "Help me!"

Zack reached around behind him to try to hold on to his butt. He knew that losing his butt not only meant losing the shield that stood between him and outer space, but it also meant losing the best butt a boy could ever have wanted.

Zack grabbed hold of his butt's hand. "I've got you," he said.

But the pull of the brown hole was overwhelming. Zack could feel his butt slipping from his grasp.

"Jump!" yelled Eleanor, standing up behind Zack.

"But it's not safe!" said Zack, one arm still hugging the giant mutant zombie blowfly's back. It was all he had left.

"Not safe?" said Eleanor. "If we stay on this giant mutant zombie blowfly, we're going to be sucked into a brown hole, you idiot!"

"You're the idiot," said Zack. "If we jump, we're going to be sucked into a brown hole anyway!"

"Language, you two!" called Gran from somewhere up in front of them.

Gran's words jolted Zack. Even in the face of a brown hole she was still fighting for the standards of decency that she held so dear. Fighting a losing battle, perhaps, but fighting nonetheless. Zack felt ashamed of himself. There was still time to make a difference. Not much time — and perhaps not much of a difference — but there was still time.

"All right!" said Zack, looking up at Eleanor. "Abandon giant mutant zombie blowfly!"

"Spoken like a true butt-fighter!" said Eleanor.

Zack stood up and, holding his butt in one hand and Eleanor's hand in the other, jumped.

Not a moment too soon.

Floating in space, Zack and Eleanor watched in awe as the Great White Butt charged toward the brown hole, followed by the giant mutant zombie blowfly they had just been riding on.

"Gran!" yelled Zack, horrified as he realized what was happening.

"Good-bye, Zack!" he heard her call. "May your butt be with you!"

"I will," called Zack's butt. "I promise."

And then, just when it seemed certain that Gran and the Great White Butt had reached the point of no return, the Great White Butt changed course. It swung across the mouth of the brown hole, turned around, and began to fly back toward Zack and Eleanor.

The giant mutant zombie blowflies, however, were nowhere near as smart — or as powerful — as the Great White Butt. Unable to escape the brown hole's gravitational pull, the entire swarm disappeared in an instant.

"So that was the Great White Butt's plan!" said Zack, watching as it battled the brown hole's gravity. "Brilliant!"

"Maybe," said Eleanor. "Maybe not."

"What do you mean?" said Zack.

"It's not out of trouble yet," said Eleanor.

Zack looked again.

Eleanor was right.

The Great White Butt was definitely struggling. It had obviously underestimated the power of the brown hole. It seemed to have reached a point where it wasn't being sucked back into it, but neither could it break free and move forward.

It was stuck.

Zack and Eleanor, still floating in space, looked at each other. They both knew that with one combined kick they could send the Great White Butt hurtling into the brown hole.

But it wasn't that straightforward.

Now that they no longer had a giant mutant zombie blowfly to ride, they had no way of moving themselves through space.

And, besides, the Great White Butt was still holding Gran.

"Help me," said the Great White Butt. "Help me and I'll let your grandmother go free!"

"Don't you dare, Zack!" said Gran.

"But, Gran!" said Zack.

"But Gran nothing!" said Gran. "You'll never get a better chance to get rid of the Great White Butt. I'm old. I've had a good life. It will be an honor to accompany the Great White Butt to its doom!"

"Don't listen to her, Zack," said the Great White Butt. "She's delirious. And she's all the family you have left. Better save her while you still have the chance."

Zack bit his lip.

"Don't listen to the Great White Butt, Zack," said Eleanor. "Maybe your gran's right. Better her than put the whole world at risk!"

"But she's my gran!" said Zack, pulling the ketchup bottle out of his belt and blowing into it.

"What are you doing?" said Eleanor. "There's no ketchup left!"

"I know that," said Zack, pointing the bottle behind them and squeezing hard. "But I don't need ketchup. I'm using it as a thruster!"

They shot toward the Great White Butt.

Zack grabbed hold of Gran's hand and wrenched her free.

Then he and Eleanor kicked the Great White Butt as hard as they could.

The enormous butt went hurtling backward into the brown hole — but not before grabbing Zack's and Eleanor's legs.

Zack, who was holding on to his gran and his butt, released both of them. But neither of them would let go.

"What are you doing?" said Zack.

"We're a team, remember?" said his butt.

"All for one and one for all!" said Gran, taking Eleanor's hand. "Right, Eleanor?"

"Right!" said Eleanor.

"Well, isn't this nice," said the Great White Butt cheerfully, as the brown hole roared and swirled around them. "Unfortunately this is where I must leave you. Enjoy your trip! And don't forget to send me a postcard!"

"That won't be necessary," said Eleanor. "You're coming with us!"

"No," said the Great White Butt. "I have a world to rule."

"Dream on!" snorted Zack's butt. "You were struggling to escape the brown hole before. What makes you think you can do it now?"

"I wasn't struggling," said the Great White Butt. "It was only an act . . . and you fell for it!" The Great White Butt let go of Zack and Eleanor and began to reverse-thrust its way back out of the brown hole.

"There's plenty more butt-fighters where we came from," said Zack. "Even if you do survive, you'll never succeed!"

"I wouldn't be so sure of that!" said the Great White

Butt. "Who's left to fight me now? A couple of geriatric has-beens! At last, Earth is mine!"

"The Forker and the Flicker are not geriatric has-beens," said Gran. "They've still got plenty of tricks up their sleeves!"

"Well, they can't help you now," said the Great White Butt. "Nothing can and nobody will!"

"I wouldn't be so sure of that!" said a voice from behind them.

Zack turned his head.

It was the Forker!

He was riding a butt that was wearing a small cardboard crown. The Prince!

"Greetings, Master!" said the Prince.

"You?" said the Great White Butt. "I thought I fed you and your friend to the maggots."

"You tried to," said the Prince. "But they weren't hungry. Too full of zombie butts."

"Never mind," said the Great White Butt. "The brown hole is ALWAYS hungry."

"Well, let's give it something to chew on," said the Forker.

"What?" said the Great White Butt.

"YOU!" said the Forker, plunging his fork deep into the Great White Butt's cheek. Then, with a mighty effort, he drew the fork — with the Great White Butt attached — up over his shoulder and catapulted it back toward the brown hole.

"Forktastic!" yelled Gran.

Zack watched as the Great White Butt hurtled past them.

It couldn't possibly recover now, he thought.

But it did.

With another enormous reverse-thrust, the Great White Butt managed to defy the brown hole yet again, bringing itself to a halt . . . right in front of Zack, Gran, Eleanor, and Zack's butt.

Zack realized what they had to do. He signaled to the others. Eleanor, Gran, and his butt nodded.

They leaned back and gave the Great White Butt a spectacular eight-legged power-kick. Zack smiled. He wished the Kicker had been there to see it.

Under the force of the kick, the Great White Butt tumbled deep into the brown hole, roaring with fury.

Zack watched the Great White Butt getting smaller and smaller as it spiraled toward its doom. He couldn't quite believe that it wasn't somehow going to pull a devious last-minute escape. After all, it *was* the Great White Butt . . . indestructible *and* immortal . . .

But then, quite suddenly, the Great White Butt vanished.

"It's a goal!" yelled Eleanor, beaming and high-fiving Zack.

"Um, I hate to be a party pooper," said Zack's butt, "but *we're* still being sucked into the hole!"

Zack, his butt, Eleanor, and Gran — still all holding hands — gulped.

"Help us, Forker!" called Zack.

The Forker rode the Prince in as close to them as he dared.

"Hang on!" he said, quickly reassembling the megafork and pushing it toward them. He hooked it around

Zack's butt-fighting belt and tried to pull them beyond the brown hole's gravitational field, but it was a struggle. Against the power of the brown hole and the combined weight of the butt-fighters, it didn't stand a chance.

"Get us out of here!" said the Forker, digging a fork into the Prince.

"Hey!" said the Prince. "Don't jab that thing in me!"

"Then hurry up!" yelled the Forker.

"They're too heavy!" said the Prince. "I can't do it!"

"Oops," said the Forker as they were dragged into the deadly vortex. "I hope the Flicker gets here soon. Otherwise we're going to be in serious trouble."

As he spoke, the Flicker arrived astride Maurice.

"Sorry," said the Flicker. "We took a wrong turn at the Moon."

"It was my fault and I'm very sorry," said Maurice. "Very, very, very, very, very —"

"Shut up, Maurice," said the Prince. "Just get us out of here!"

"Language!" said Gran.

The Flicker didn't mess around. He stood on Maurice and quickly knotted a string of towels together. Then, with a few deft flicks of his wrist, he transformed the string into an enormous lasso, and cast it around the group of struggling butt-fighters.

"Never fear, the Flicker's here!" said the Flicker as he jerked the lasso tight and began pulling them to safety.

"Hey!" said Gran. "That's my catchphrase!"

"But I don't have one of my own," said the Flicker.

"All right," said Gran. "You can use it just this once."

"And never, never, never fear, Maurice is also at your

service!" said Maurice as he sweated and strained to help the Flicker.

"That's pathetic," said the Prince. "It doesn't even rhyme."

"Catchphrases don't have to rhyme," said the Forker.

"But it's better if they do," said the Prince. "It's what makes then catchy."

"Sorry, Prince," said Maurice. "I'm very, very, very —"

"Shut up, Maurice," said the Prince.

"Language!" said Gran.

"Shut up is not a swear word," said the Prince.

"It's not a nice word," said Gran.

Eleanor smiled at Zack.

He smiled back. Things were already getting back to normal and they weren't even home yet. Zack glanced over his shoulder into the brown hole.

And then he stopped smiling.

The brown hole seemed to be swirling faster than ever.

Swirling and . . .

and . . .

EXPANDING!

Despite having eaten an entire swarm of giant mutant zombie blowflies *and* the Great White Butt, it seemed that the brown hole was still not satisfied.

Zack realized the terrible truth.

They weren't going to get out after all.

CHAPTER FIFTEEN

Beyond the Brown Hole

Zack closed his eyes.

The sucking noise increased to a deafening roar. He felt himself being stretched to the breaking point and then . . .

. . . Zack opened his eyes and looked around him.

He, his butt, and Eleanor were hurtling through space. He had no idea where they were or how much time had passed. All he knew was that they had been sucked into a brown hole.

Zack wondered why he was still thinking.

Or breathing, for that matter.

Hadn't his butt's bubble shield broken up?

By rights he should have been dead.

Unless he was indestructible, of course, which — as far as he knew — was not the case. He definitely hadn't been zombie-buttified. Sure, he'd breathed in some of the smoke that came from the Forker's incinerator, but . . .

That was it!

The zombie butts were virtually indestructible.

The zombie butt smoke he and the others had inhaled must have given them some sort of immunity from the effects of being in space. But judging by how bad Zack felt, it wasn't perfect. And there was no telling how much longer it would last.

He realized the Blind Butt-feeler had been right all along. The hokeypokey and the ketchup and the brown hole had all helped to save the world.

What the Blind Butt-feeler hadn't told him, however, was at what cost.

He'd lost his parents.

He'd lost his gran.

And now he was lost in space and about to lose his own life along with his butt and Eleanor.

The Blind Butt-feeler had told Zack that he had a long and difficult road ahead of him. But she hadn't told him just how long or how difficult that road would be. Or that it would lead to a dead end.

Zack reached out and touched Eleanor's arm.

"What's going to happen to us?" said Zack. "Do you think we'll just hurtle through space forever?"

Eleanor nodded grimly. "It's highly likely. Unless we hit something. Or something causes us to change direction."

Zack was suddenly filled with hope. He looked at his butt. Maybe . . .

"Don't look at me," said his butt. "I'm all out of gas. That bubble shield really took it out of me."

Zack nodded and clutched at his throat.

He could feel his body fluids beginning to boil. He could feel bubbles forming in his blood. He could feel the gases in his body beginning to expand. He could feel his thoughts slowing down.

"Zack," said Eleanor. "You've got steam coming out of your ears."

"So have you," he said.

"But of course," said Eleanor, putting her hand on her hip and breaking into song. "I'm a little teapot, short and stout . . ."

Zack felt really sick. Eleanor's mind was going. It was an ugly sight, despite the fact that she seemed to be enjoying herself — in fact the fact that she was enjoying herself just seemed to make it even worse.

"Here is my handle, here is my spout . . ." she sang, putting her right arm out like a teapot spout.

"When I get all steamed up, then I SHOUT . . ."

Zack couldn't bear it anymore. Watching Eleanor — once a proud and fierce butt-fighting warrior — reduced to a singing teapot somehow seemed to be the saddest thing of all on a day of extremely sad things.

"TIP ME OVER . . . POUR ME OUT!" sang Eleanor. "Come on, Zack, join in!"

Zack looked away as Eleanor began the song again, this time accompanied by his butt.

He knew it wouldn't be long before he was singing, too.

But he was determined to hold out for as long as possible.

He wondered where they were. A little way back he had recognized Saturn. That meant they must have already passed Jupiter. Zack tried to remember what the next planet out from Saturn was.

And then, far off in the distance, he saw it.

At first it was no bigger than a golf ball.

A brown golf ball.

But they were traveling so fast that the brown golf ball rapidly expanded to the size of a brown tennis ball, which rapidly expanded to the size of a brown basketball, which rapidly expanded to the size of a brown beach ball, which rapidly expanded to the size of a brown planet.

Zack smiled as he suddenly remembered the name of the next planet out from Saturn.

Uranus!

It was no longer blue — in fact, it looked more like a piece of fruit that had been left out in the sun — but it was Uranus all right. It wasn't just the twelve moons that gave it away either. It was the smell.

"I must be the luckiest butt-fighter in the univarse," said Zack to nobody in particular as they began a rapid descent toward the planet's surface. "Either that, or the unluckiest."

He wrapped a fluffy pink toilet seat cover around his head, closed his eyes, and prepared to find out.

●● ●● ●●

They hit the soft sludge of Uranus with three loud squelches.

Zack, curled up like a baby at the bottom of a sludgy hole, could hear his name being called.

He opened his eyes. They were burning from the incredible stench, but he could make out the shape of his butt hovering above him.

"Zack!" it called. "Are you okay?"

Zack nodded. He stood and looked up to the top of the hole. "How do I get out of here?" he asked.

"I'll come down and pull you out," said his butt.

"But I thought you were out of gas," said Zack.

"I was," said his butt, "but Uranus is full of methane. I'm completely recharged."

Zack coughed, not sure if his butt being completely recharged with methane was entirely a good thing, but he was pleased to see it looking so well.

His butt gently descended and extended its arm to him. Zack grabbed it and his butt lifted him to the surface.

Zack stood and looked around. He saw a featureless brown landscape. "So this is Uranus," he said.

"I'm sorry," said his butt. "I didn't realize it was so obvious."

"I meant the planet," said Zack.

"Oh," said his butt, "I thought you meant . . ."

"Quiet!" said Zack. "What's that?"

"What's what?" said his butt.

"Sounds like singing," said Zack. "Listen!"

"Humpty Dumpty sat on a wall . . ." sang a familiar voice.

It was coming from another hole close by.

"It's Eleanor," said Zack.

They waded across to the edge of the nearby hole. Eleanor was lying at the bottom, her space madness apparently compounded by full-blown methane madness.

"Humpty Dumpty had a BIG FALL . . ." she sang.

Zack looked around them grimly. His relief at surviving the impact with Uranus and happiness at having found his butt and Eleanor was rapidly being replaced by a new worry.

"All the king's horses and all the king's men . . . COULDN'T PUT HUMPTY TOGETHER AGAIN!" sang Eleanor as Zack's butt airlifted her to the surface.

The words of the nursery rhyme sent shivers down Zack's spine.

There was no escaping the reality of their situation. Sure, Uranus had stopped their potentially infinite head-long tumble through space, but all the king's horses and all the king's men couldn't get them back to Earth again.

They were going to die on Uranus.

Just like his parents.

Zack felt tears come into his eyes. He hadn't even had a chance to say good-bye. He had to find them. Wiping his eyes, Zack scanned the horizon.

"What are you looking for, Zack?" said his butt.

"My parents," said Zack. They must be around here somewhere!"

"But they're dead, Zack," said his butt.

"I know that," said Zack, sniffing, "but the least we can do is to bury them before we die as well. Can I stand on top of you?"

"No," said his butt as Zack jumped on top of it.

Zack peered as far into the distance as he could.

Uranus was a big planet. While nowhere near as huge as Jupiter or Saturn, and even though it had lost a large part of its mass in the collision with the Great White Butt, it was still at least ten times as big as Earth. The chance that Zack had landed anywhere near his parents was infinitesimally small.

But it was still a chance.

He heard Eleanor again.

"Three blind mice, three blind mice," she sang. "See how they run, see how they run . . ."

A flash of yellow caught Zack's eye. "What's that?" he said.

"What's what?" said his butt.

"That!" said Zack.

"What?" said his butt.

"That yellow thing!" said Zack.

"I can't see anything!" said his butt. "You're standing on top of me, remember?"

Zack saw that Eleanor had a pair of buttoculars attached to her belt. He jumped down off his butt, grabbed them, and jumped back up.

Raising the buttoculars to his eyes he could see the clear outline of a butt-mobile.

Two figures in spacesuits were draped over the front of it.

"Let's go," said Zack.

●● ●● ●●

Zack waded through the stinking sludge of Uranus toward his parents.

Eleanor trailed along behind, still singing, "Ring around the rosey . . . a pocket full of posies . . ."

Zack wished she would stop. She was giving him the creeps.

"Shut up, Eleanor!" he said.

242

But Eleanor just looked at him through glazed eyes and continued her song. "Ashes, ashes, WE ALL FALL DOWN!"

At this she kicked her legs out from underneath her and fell down into the sludge. Zack and his butt fished her out. She was covered in sludge, but still singing.

And so they proceeded.

They finally reached the half-buried butt-mobile. Zack could smell his mother's perfume, the fumes obviously left over from the perfume bomb. The two bodies on top of the butt-mobile betrayed no signs of life.

"Mom?" he called. "Dad?"

There was no response.

He climbed up the ladder.

He gasped at the sight in front of him.

His mother and father were both lying on their backs with their hands clutching their throats. They reeked of perfume and the sinister stench of the Great White Butt.

Zack rushed to his mother's side.

Despite the coldness of the atmosphere, she was still warm.

So was his father.

Zack's heart skipped a beat.

He knelt beside his mother and tried to remember how to perform emergency heart massage.

"What are you doing, Zack?" said his butt. "They're dead."

"They're still warm," said Zack, crossing his hands over his mother's chest and pushing down hard. "Maybe I can resuscitate them."

Zack's butt nodded. "Do you want me to give them butt-to-mouth resuscitation?"

"No," said Zack, pushing down with all his might. "I think that will make things worse. Let's just try to start their hearts. I'll work on Mom, you start on Dad."

Zack's butt climbed onto James Freeman's chest and started bouncing up and down as if it were on a trampoline.

They continued for a full five minutes.

But there was no response from either James or Judi.

"It's okay," said Zack to his butt. "You can stop. It's no use."

"Oops," said his butt, which was a little too full of methane for its own good. "Beg your pardon."

Zack coughed.

Eleanor coughed.

And then, most amazing of all, James and Judi Freeman coughed.

"Mom? Dad?" said Zack. "You're alive!"

"Zack?" said his mother, sitting up.

"Zack?" said his father, blinking and confused.

Zack threw his arms around them both, all of them crying with relief and happiness. "I can't believe you're okay!" said Zack.

"Neither can I, to tell you the truth," said James. "The Great White Butt blasted us, but your mother managed to set off a perfume bomb at the same time. The bomb neutralized most of his stench, but the force of the blast must have knocked us out."

They hugged again. Zack's butt joined in the hug as well.

"Strange," it said, "but I feel like you're my parents, too!"

Zack's father immediately broke out of the hug and reached for his nail-gun. "You're dead meat, butt!"

"No!" said Zack. "It's my butt! It's on our side!"

"But I don't understand," said his father. "How can a butt be on our side? And what are you doing here anyway?"

"I don't know where to begin," said Zack. "There's kind of a lot to explain."

Eleanor cleared her throat. "You can say that again!" she said. "What happened? Where are we? I remember flying through space, and then it gets a bit blurry, but there was something about a teapot . . ."

"Well, aren't you going to introduce us to your friend?" said Zack's mother.

"You mean his *girl*friend," said Zack's butt.

"I am NOT his girlfriend," said Eleanor, landing a solid kick in the middle of Zack's butt.

"Ouch!" said Zack's butt.

"Ouch!" said Zack.

"It asked for it," said Eleanor.

"Mom and Dad," said Zack, "I'd like you to meet Eleanor Sterne. Eleanor, these are my parents."

"Eleanor Sterne?" said James Freeman, shaking her hand. "Silas Sterne's daughter? It's a great honor! He never stops talking about you. How is he?"

Eleanor bit her lip. "I don't know," she said. "When we left him, he was zombie-buttified. We had to lock him in a butt-fighting simulator. We haven't seen him since the start of the zombie buttvasion."

"Zombie buttvasion!" said James, slowly recovering his memory. "How bad is it?"

"Relax," said Zack. "The situation is under control. It was touch and go for a while, but we got rid of them."

"And the Great White Butt?" said Judi. "It said it was going back to kill you!"

"He won't be giving anybody any more trouble," said Zack. "Thanks to Gran."

"Gran!?" said James. "What did she have to do with it?"

"Everything," said Zack, his voice wavering, and unable to hold back his tears any longer. "Everything."

●● ●● ●●

By the time Zack had finished telling his parents the whole story, not one of the butt-fighters — or even Zack's butt — had a dry eye.

Zack's mother held him by the shoulders. "I'm proud of you, Zack, and your gran would be, too. You've achieved so much," she said, "but how? You failed the Junior Butt-fighters' League entrance exam three times."

"I don't know," said Zack. "I guess I'm just not good at exams."

Zack's dad put his hand on Zack's shoulder. "Let's go home, son."

"Great idea, Dad," said Zack.

Zack's dad winced. "One problem . . ." he said. "Our butt-mobile's stuck. The methane tanks are full, but it's buried a little too deep."

Zack's butt jumped up. "No problem!" it said. "You

just need a little extra thrust. And I'm just the butt to provide it! Tie me down, Zack."

Zack climbed up and lashed his butt to the back of the butt-mobile with reinforced toilet paper.

"Ready when you are!" it said.

"That's one doozy of a butt you've got there, boy," said James.

"Yeah," said Zack, patting his butt. "It's a good one, all right. If it was self-wiping it'd be perfect!"

"I don't need to be self-wiping," said Zack's butt. "That's what I've got you for!"

CHAPTER SIXTEEN

Graduation Day

Powered by both the pure Uranusian methane and Zack's butt, James and Judi Freeman's butt-mobile broke all known space-travel speed records on its way back to Earth.

As they flew they saw the brown hole in the distance.

"There it is," announced James. "Just look at that monster!"

Zack shuddered as he stared at it.

Even from this great distance Zack was aware of its dizzying power. He felt himself being drawn into it. His brain seemed to be swirling in his skull — churning and spinning like the brown hole itself. And, as his brain and the brown hole seemed to merge, Zack became aware of a sort of wordless understanding between them. An understanding that there was unfinished business between them. "You'll be back," it seemed to be whispering to him. "You'll be back."

As Zack stared out of the butt-mobile porthole he felt his mother's hand on his shoulder.

The whirling in Zack's brain subsided, and he and his mother gazed out the window together as the brown hole receded into the distance.

"Zack," said Judi, "I want you to know that I hope you will continue your butt-fighting career, if that's what you want to do."

Zack nodded. "Thanks, Mom," he said.

"But you must promise me one thing," she said.

"Sure, Mom," said Zack, still trying to make sense of what had just happened. "What is it?"

"You must promise me that you will never go near a brown hole again!" she said.

"I didn't exactly go into that one on purpose," said Zack.

Judi Freeman put a finger across her son's lips. "Listen to me, Zack," she said. "Brown holes are terrible and dangerous things and should be avoided at all costs. You might have gotten lucky this time, but normally not even the most experienced, most skilled butt-fighters stand a snowball's chance in hell of surviving a first — let alone second — encounter with one of those monsters."

Zack tried hard not to smile. Silas Sterne must have given the same lecture on interplanetary butt-fighting every year since the beginning of the univarse. He didn't doubt that Silas Sterne was telling the truth — at least the truth as he knew it — but he wondered if it was the whole truth. Zack couldn't help wondering why — out of all the places they could possibly have landed — the brown hole had deposited them on Uranus at almost exactly the same spot where his parents were. He couldn't explain it, but it seemed more than just coincidence. Zack suspected that the univarse was perhaps more mysterious than Silas Sterne — or indeed anyone — had dared to imagine.

Despite these thoughts, however, Zack nodded solemnly as his mother continued. "Because make no mistake, Zack," she said. "That is what they are! Monsters! They'll suck you in and chew you up!"

"Yes, Mom," said Zack.

"Don't 'Yes, Mom' me!" said Judi. "Just promise me on your honor that you will NEVER go near one EVER again for ANY reason."

Zack nodded, feeling the weight of the moment. "Okay, Mom," he said. "I promise."

"Good," Judi said, relaxing a little. "Good boy."

●● ●● ●●

The butt-mobile touched down smoothly on the Butt-fighting Academy landing strip exactly one week later at 0900 hours Earth time. James taxied to the terminal and shut down the engine.

Despite having sustained massive zombie buttvasion damage, most of the buildings on the butt-mobile port were still standing. Normally at this time of the morning, it would have been busy with trainee butt-fighter butt-mobile pilots practicing takeoffs, landings, and midair maneuvers, but today it was deserted.

Zack opened the hatch, climbed out, and untied his butt from the back of the butt-mobile.

It was shivering and exhausted, but otherwise okay.

"Thanks," said Zack, holding his butt up to his face. "You did a great job. I know we haven't always seen eye to eye, but you really came through for me. I'm proud to have a butt like you."

"And I'm proud to be your butt," it said. "Now shut up and reattach me: I'm freezing!"

Zack smiled and pushed his butt down the back of his pants. "I'll have you warmed up in no time," he said.

Zack looked up and saw Eleanor watching him. As soon as he caught her eye she glanced away.

"Can you hear music?" said James.

"Yes," said Judi. "It's coming from the chapel."

"Let's go check it out," said James. "But be careful. And be quiet. We have to make sure there are no zombie butts left. It could be a trap."

Eleanor, Zack, and Judi nodded.

They armed themselves with butt-guns and crept up the hill.

What they saw at the top amazed them.

The Butt Hunter, the Kicker, the Smacker, and all of the Academy's trainee butt-fighters were there. The front of the chapel seemed to be buried in flowers.

"What's happening?" whispered Zack.

"Looks like a funeral," said Eleanor, smiling.

"Who for?" said Zack.

"Us," said Eleanor.

"Us?" said Zack. "But we're not dead."

"Yeah," said Eleanor. "I know that. And you know that. But they don't know that."

"Shouldn't we tell them we're here?" said Zack.

"And spoil the surprise?" said James. "Not on your life! Besides, it's not often you get to attend your own funeral!"

As they crept up closer to the front of the chapel, the music stopped. The Kicker stood up and addressed the congregation.

"I'm a man of few words, but Silas has asked me to say a bit about Zack Freeman — one of our dear departed comrades for whom we have gathered here today to remember — and I'm very proud to do so."

The Kicker paused.

The cadets were silent.

"I'm going to be honest," said the Kicker. "When I first met Zack Freeman, I didn't see a butt-fighter. All I saw was a frightened and confused little boy. And a clumsy one at that. But, by the toes of my favorite kicking boots, did that frightened, confused, and clumsy boy learn fast!

"Not only did he defeat Stenchgantor single-handedly with nothing more than a pair of smelly socks, but he fired a harpoon into the Great White Butt and then, as if these services to humanity weren't enough for one boy — for one lifetime — he risked his life to save the world by lighting a match inside a fully loaded buttcano!

"In the process he came to earn himself a nomination for the Butt Hunters' Hall of Fame — the youngest person ever to be nominated for such an honor — and he achieved this without even having earned his elementary butt-fighter's certificate."

At this the cadets burst into applause. In fact, it was all Zack could do to stop himself from applauding as well. It was difficult to believe that the Kicker was talking about him and not somebody else.

"After that," said the Kicker, "Zack came here, to the Academy, to study for that butt-fighter's certificate, and it is here that I must make a confession. We butt-fighters are trained to not make mistakes, but I made a terrible one. One that I will never forgive myself for as long as I live."

The Kicker's voice was wavering. The Smacker put her hand on his shoulder. The Kicker took a deep breath and continued.

"Zack quit the course after only a few weeks, believing himself to be a failure because he was unable to complete routine simulated butt-fighting missions. But the fault was not his, it was mine. After returning from the buttcano, I broke the first rule of butt-fighting: I forgot to wash my hands. As a consequence, I believe I picked up some sort of infection. I haven't been feeling one hundred percent for some weeks and I can now see that during that time I made a terrible error.

"Believing I had set the simulator on the basic level of difficulty — which was appropriate for Zack at that stage of his training — I didn't realize until he'd left that I'd mistakenly set it for the most extreme level of difficulty possible. Far from failing the simulated missions, ladies and gentlemen, it was a wonder that he managed to survive any of them for as long as he did. He didn't deserve my condemnation — in fact not only did Zack easily complete the requirements for his butt-fighter's certificate, but he also deserves a special medal of excellence of simulated butt-fighting achievement."

"Well done, son," whispered James, patting Zack on the back.

"We're proud of you," whispered Judi.

"I told you you were a butt-fighter!" said Eleanor.

"I helped, too," said Zack's butt, but nobody was paying it any attention. They were all looking at Zack.

Zack, however, couldn't speak. He was in a state of shock. To have been sucked into a brown hole and survived was one thing. But to go from the bottom of the class to the top was something else altogether.

"Who knows what the potential of this boy might have been?" said the Kicker. "Had he continued his training here he might have acquired the extra skills he needed to survive his clearly fatal encounter with the zombie butts from Uranus."

The Kicker's voice was cracking badly now, but he was determined to get to the end. "I can only ask his forgiveness," said the Kicker, "and present him, posthumously with this certificate and this medal . . ."

"Go get it!" said Eleanor, digging Zack in the ribs. "You've earned it!"

Zack grinned. He got to his feet and walked to the front of the chapel. "I believe those are mine," he said to the Kicker.

There was a collective gasp from the congregation.

"Zack?" said the Kicker. "You're alive!" He threw his arms around Zack. "Can you ever forgive me, boy?"

"Are you kidding?" said Zack. "You saved my life. Without experience of butt-fighting at that level, I wouldn't have stood a chance!"

"Spoken like a true butt-fighter!" said the Kicker, handing him the certificate and pinning the medal to his vest.

Zack shook the Kicker's hand and turned to face the congregation. "I'd like to dedicate these awards to three of the best and bravest butt-fighters I've ever known: the Forker, the Flicker, and the Pincher." He looked up into the sky, tears rolling down his cheeks. "These are for you, Gran — wherever you are."

The congregation bowed their heads in respectful silence.

Meanwhile, James and Judi, followed by Eleanor, moved to the front of the chapel to comfort Zack. They were quickly joined by the Smacker, Silas Sterne — and even Mittens — for one enormous group hug.

● ● ●

"Dad!" said Eleanor, kissing Silas's face. "I'm so sorry we had to lock you all in the simulator!"

"Are you kidding?" bellowed Silas, wrapping Eleanor in a bear hug. "We had a GREAT time! Three days of nonstop virtual butt-fighting! Of course, nothing beats the real thing, eh, boy?" said Silas, nudging Zack.

"You're right about that, sir!" said Zack, beaming with pride.

"But what about the zombie butts that attached themselves to you?" said Eleanor. "How did they get out of the simulator?"

"They didn't," said the Smacker.

"But," said Eleanor, flashing an alarmed glance at Zack, "then that means . . ."

"Don't worry," said Silas. "They're not going to hurt anybody where they are."

"But where are they?" said Eleanor.

The Smacker laughed. "They melted in the heat of the simulated buttcano," she said. "Gave off a terrible stink. I took in a lungful or two, but you know I've never felt better in my whole life!"

"I know exactly what you mean!" said Eleanor, nodding.

"Just do me a favor," said Silas. "Next time you lock us in a simulator for days on end, don't forget to leave us some FOOD! We almost tore one another apart until we found a stockpile of virtual anti-butt energy bars."

Before Zack could ask Silas how they could possibly melt zombie butts with simulated heat and survive on simulated food, his father came up and slapped Silas on the back. "And how about you do me a favor," said James. "Next time you decide to leave us all alone on Uranus," said James, "well, just DON'T!"

"Sorry about that," said Silas, "but when you've gotta go, you've gotta go!"

James, Judi, and Silas laughed.

Zack looked at the certificate in his hands.

"You've got to be happy with that, Zack," said Eleanor. "Congratulations."

"Thanks," said Zack, "but I'd be happier if I knew what happened to my gran."

Eleanor nodded. "It's really hard, Zack, I know, but try not to worry too much. Your gran is one tough old butt-fighter. Whatever happened and wherever she is, I reckon she'll be able to look after herself. I pity any butts that get in her way, though."

"Do you think there are butts in other parts of the univarse?" said Zack.

"I don't know," said Eleanor. "But if there are, I'm sure Mabel and her Angels will whip them into shape."

"Yeah," said Zack, wiping a tear from his eye. "I think you're probably right."

At that moment Zack's butt — who tended to get bored at formal occasions — did a long, loud fart.

"Looks like you could use a hand whipping this butt into shape," laughed Eleanor, wiping a tear from her own eye.

"Lay a finger on me and I'll blast you from here to Uranus!" said Zack's butt.

"Language!" said Zack, smiling.

THE END

Epilogue

There are many theories about what happens to matter when it is sucked inside a brown hole, but the truth is most of the theories are just that. Theories. All that can be said for sure is that there is a very strong possibility that the forces inside a brown hole are powerful enough to form wormholes in the fabric of the universe — wormholes powerful enough to allow vast interstellar distances to be traveled in the blink of an eye, or even, perhaps, powerful enough to permit time travel.

from *The Origins of the Univarse* by Sir Roger Francis Rectum, Smellbourne University Press, 2002

Glossary

Abuminable Brownman
The older, browner, and much smellier brother of the *Abominable Snowman*.

Abominable Snowman
The younger, whiter, and much less smelly brother of the *Abuminable Brownman*.

Anti-butt energy bars
Favorite food of *butt-fighters*. They inhibit the sense of smell and contain massive amounts of protein for extra smacking, kicking, kissing, flicking, pinching, and forking power.

Atomic butt
Just like an atomic bomb, except browner. And smellier. And MUCH more dangerous. Not to be approached —

unless you are a qualified atomic butt disposal expert, in which case you should dismantle and dispose of it thoughtfully in the nearest garbage can.

Atomic pinch
A pinch delivered to a butt, or butts, that has been compressed to bursting point.

Blind Butt-feeler, the
The person with the power to "read" butts and reveal amazing — but frequently mystifying — information about the past, present, and future.

Buttswana
African country. Scene of the Great Butt Uprising of 1998 in which the Kisser was buttnapped and switched allegiances to the butts. See also *The Netherlands, Buttbay, Smellbourne*, the *Moon, Uranus.*

Brown holes
Very similar to black holes except brown. They are formed when vast interstellar butts run out of gas and collapse under the power of their own repulsive stench, which reverses itself and endows the newly formed brown holes with the power to suck anything and everything into themselves. Nobody knows what happens to matter sucked into a brown hole, but there is a strong possibility that the forces inside a brown hole are strong enough to form wormholes in the fabric of the univarse — wormholes powerful enough to allow vast interstellar

distances to be traveled in the blink of an eye or even, perhaps, to permit time travel.

B-Team, the
A crack butt-fighting unit made up of the *Kicker*, the *Smacker*, and the *Kisser*.

Buttbardment
A bombardment consisting exclusively of butts. Avoid if possible but, if caught, seek nearest butt shelter.

Buttbay
Very similar to Bombay in India except browner. And smellier. Avoid visiting if at all possible. See also *The Netherlands*, *Buttswana*, *Smellbourne*, the *Moon*, *Uranus*.

Butt-blitz
Ground, sea, or air attack by two or more butts.

Buttcano
An extinct volcano colonized by butts. Avoid.

Buttcatcher
Person employed by the local council to catch lost or runaway butts.

Buttmergency
An emergency situation created by butts.

Butt-fighter
Any individual engaged in butt-resistance, either in a paid or voluntary capacity.

Butt-fighting simulator
Virtual-reality machine invented by Silas Sterne to simulate a wide range of butt-fighting environments and challenges used for training rookie butt-fighters. The simulator is so powerful that users forget they are in a simulated environment and actually believe that they are fighting butts.

Butt-fighters' Retirement Home
See *retired butt-fighters' rest home*.

Butt-gun
All-purpose, anti-butt weapon. Fires a wide variety of ammunition, including thumbtacks, staples, and rusty nails.

Butt Hunter
A butt-warrior who has given up regular butt-fighting in order to concentrate his or her energies on hunting big-game butts. This occupation is so fraught with danger that only a few of the bravest, most talented, and smartest Butt Hunters survive.

Butt Hunters' Hall of Fame
A museum dedicated to preserving and honoring the exploits of great *butt hunters* and *butt-fighters*.

Buttination
Domination of a place — or entire planet — by butts.

Butt-mobile
Multipurpose all-terrain butt-fighting vehicle.

Buttnapped
To be kidnapped by butts.

Buttnappers
Butts that buttnap.

Buttoculars
A device that employs *infra-brown* technology to allow a viewer to see butts at a great distance.

Bumper Book of Butts, The
The definitive work on butts, much favored by butt-fighters. As well as being a general reference guide containing many useful facts about butts, it also has a full selection of butt-hunting maps, butt identification charts, sections on how to defend yourself against butts, how to catch and tame feral butts, how to hunt big butts, and how to stock a butt-hunting arsenal.

Butt-piranha
A carnivorous butt-fish found in shallow areas of the Sea of Butts and simulated rivers.

Buttoline
A trampoline formed by using the natural sponginess of buttocks.

Buttquake
Just like an earthquake, only wobblier. And smellier.

Buttvasion
Invasion of a place — or entire planet — by butts.

Buttzilla
Enormous fire-farting butt fond of destroying large cities and fighting other enormous fire-farting butts.

Crapalanche
Just like an avalanche except crappier. And browner. And smellier.

E-mission
Task or project undertaken by a *butt-fighter*. Not to be confused with "emission" which is something else entirely (see *"fart"*).

E-Mission Control
Main command center for coordinating all butt-fighting E-missions.

Fart
A small — or large — cloud of gas.

FBBI
Federal Bureau of Butt Intelligence.

Flicker, the
Legendary butt-fighter highly skilled in the art of towel-to-butt combat. Member of the the world's first butt-fighting team, *Mabel's Angels*.

Fluffy pink toilet seat cover
Fluffy pink cover for covering toilet seats. Absolutely irresistible to butts. Also handy as an emergency crash helmet.

Forker, the
Legendary butt-fighter highly skilled in the art of fork-to-butt combat. Member of the world's first butt-fighting team, *Mabel's Angels*.

FORKTASTIC!
An exclamation used to express great joy when a fork hits its target, usually a butt.

Generic toilet paper
A paper product consisting of a series of perforated squares rolled around a cardboard tube. Used for smoothing the rough edges off wooden two-by-fours, sanding down benches, and torturing butts. See also *toilet paper*.

Giant mutant blowfly
Adult form of giant mutant maggot.

Giant mutant zombie blowfly
Adult form of giant mutant maggot that has feasted on zombie butts. These blowflies are virtually indestructible and should be avoided if possible.

Great White Butt, the
A rogue butt regarded by many as the most evil butt in the *univarse*. There are many theories about its origins. Some believe it to be a mutant butt created as a side-effect of nuclear testing in the Pacific. Eric von Dunnycan, in his book *Chariots of the Butts,* claimed that the Great White Butt was a space traveler who arrived on Earth thousands of years ago. Others believe the Great White Butt has been around for even longer and that it dates back 150 million years to the age of the dinosaurs.

Hokeypokey
A really stupid dance, but quite good for amusing small children. Also good for sending *zombie butts* into a mysterious trance that enables you to pretty much lead them anywhere. To be generally avoided unless you are a small child — or a parent desperately trying to amuse a small child — or your town is about to be overrun by zombie butts.

Infra-brown
Generating, using, or sensitive to the wavelength of infra-brown radiation.

Infra-brown camera
A device that employs *infra-brown* technology to allow a

viewer to photograph butts that would otherwise be invisible to the naked eye.

Ketchup
A substance with quasi-magical properties, capable of making ANYTHING taste better. Particularly useful for improving the taste of vegetables and *zombie butts*.

Kicker, the
Legendary butt-fighter highly skilled in the art of foot-to-butt combat. Member of the famous *B-team*.

Kisser, the
Exceptionally charming butt-fighter highly skilled in the art of lip-to-butt combat. Brainwashed by butts in *Buttswana,* he became a butt sympathizer and attempted to kill the other members of the *B-team*. Last seen being dragged down into a deadly brown lake by giant maggots inside a *buttcano*.

K-TEL three-six-zero PT-XR fourteen thousand and two point five HRH triple turbo automatic multispeed butt-splitter/dicer and slicer
Prototype of the "multifunction" butt-gun. Also juices but this is best avoided as the attachment is very difficult to clean.

Mabel's Angels
The world's first butt-fighting team, consisting of the *Flicker,* the *Forker,* and, founding member Mabel Freeman, the *Pincher*.

Mabeltown

Large country town named in honor of Mabel Freeman in recognition of her efforts as the founding member of *Mabel's Angels*, credited with inventing modern butt-fighting.

Maggotorium

Enormous underground chamber. The cold, dark, and moist conditions provide ideal conditions for maggots, Maggot Lords, mutant maggots, Mutant Maggot Lords, and a range of other lowdown scum-sucking parasites.

Mega-fork

An exceptionally large fork formed by assembling many smaller forks. Warning: Assembly not recommended for children under six without adult supervision.

Methane madness

Delirium caused by exposure to high levels of methane. May cause hallucinations, visions, aggression, sudden mood swings, headaches, and vomiting. Can be relieved with pure oxygen.

Moon

That big white thing you see up in the sky at night. Also used to describe the act of revealing one's buttocks unexpectedly for the purposes of shock or amusement.

Mutant maggots

Larval stage of giant blowflies that have become abnormally large as a result of prolonged exposure to the toxic environment inside a *buttcano*.

Mutant Maggot Lord, the
An exceptionally charming human being who, despite having his physical form mutated beyond recognition as a result of prolonged exposure to the extreme toxicity of a brown lake inside a *buttcano*, retains his persuasive powers.

Mutant zombie maggots
Larval stage of giant blowflies that have become abnormally large as a result of prolonged exposure to the toxic environment inside a *buttcano* as well as being *zombie-buttified* from the inside as a result of feasting on *zombie butts*. Virtually indestructible, completely uncharmable, and totally resistant to the power of the *hokeypokey*.

Nailgun Series 9000
A popular butt-gun that fires high-velocity nails at its target (usually a butt). The 9000 series was notable for the innovation of using rusty nails capable of delivering a shot of tetanus as well as intense pain.

Netherlands, The
A remote country in the vast, unchartered wilderness known as the Nether Regions. Often confused with Holland. See also *Buttbay, Buttswana, Smellbourne,* the *Moon, Uranus.*

Nostril-hairicide
A rare condition in which one's nostril hairs terminate themselves, usually in response to a particularly repugnant or overwhelming smell.

Plastic squeeze bottle
Extremely simple and efficient propulsion device for delivering *ketchup* to a specified target (usually a vegetable, but can also be used for fighting butts).

Pincher, the
Legendary butt-fighter highly skilled in the art of forefinger and thumb-to-butt combat. Founding member of the world's first butt-fighting team, *Mabel's Angels*.

Poopigator
Just like an alligator, except browner. And smellier. Avoid.

Rearrangement
A process whereby human bodies are reorganized so that butts and heads swap places. Highly sought after by butts. Highly dreaded by heads.

Retired butt-fighters' rest home
Set up by the Butt-fighters' Union to house the fortunate few *butt-fighters* who reach old age, despite the odds stacked against them by their dangerous profession.

Rhinocerarse
Just like a rhinoceros, only browner. And smellier. Avoid.

Sewagefall
Just like a waterfall except browner. And smellier. Avoid.

Silas Sterne's Butt-fighting Academy
Founded by Silas Sterne in order to give rookie *butt-fighters* a solid grounding in the theory and practice of serious butt-fighting.

Smacker, the
Legendary *butt-fighter* highly skilled in the art of hand-to-butt combat. Member of the famous *B-team*.

Smellbourne
Small city Down Under with a big stink. Home of *Zack Freeman*.

Smellbourne University Press
Courageous publishing house responsible for publishing Sir Roger Francis Rectum's controversial book, *The Origin of the Univarse*.

Soap
A *butt-fighter's* best friend. (N.B.: The first rule of butt-fighting is to always wash your hands afterwards.)

Stenchgantor
Also known as the Great Unwiped Butt, it is the ugliest, dirtiest, wartiest, pimpliest, grossest, greasiest, hairiest, stinkiest butt in the entire world. Or, at least it was, until *Zack Freeman* outstenched it with a pair of very smelly socks.

Toilet paper
A paper product consisting of a series of perforated squares rolled around a cardboard tube. Used for wiping butts. See also *Generic toilet paper.*

UFBs
See *unidentified flying butts.*

Unidentified flying butts
A flying butt that cannot be identified. What did you think it was? This isn't exactly brain surgery, you know.

Univarse
Everything that you can possibly think of plus everything that you can't. There are many theories about how the univarse began, but the truth is that most of the theories are just that. Theories. All that can be said for certain is that in the beginning there was a butt.

Uranus
1.783 billion miles from the sun. The planet has 17 known moons and 11 rings. Uranus's surface is an ocean of liquid methane that gives the planet a beautiful blue color. N.B.: Extreme caution must be taken with the pronunciation of this planet's name to avoid potential confusion and embarrassment.

Utility belt
Originally worn by a *buttcatcher* to hold all his or her butt-catching gear (e.g., *fluffy pink toilet seat cover, toilet paper,* and *soap*). Once shunned as little more than a

child's toy by *butt-fighters*, it was popularized by *Zack Freeman* and is now becoming increasingly adopted by all classes of anti-butt personnel.

Wiper, the
Legendary butt-fighter, highly skilled in the art of toilet paper-to-butt combat.

Zack's butt
Zack Freeman and his butt have a long history of disagreeing with each other. In fact, two months after his twelfth birthday, Zack was shocked to discover his runaway butt addressing a midnight butt rally in which it encouraged other butts to create a *buttcano* powerful enough to knock out every human being on the planet, so that butts could *"rearrange"* the human body to take the coveted spot on top of the neck where they felt they rightly belonged. After a long and difficult journey involving both great danger and personal sacrifice, as well as a descent into the heart of the explosive *buttcano,* Zack was able to make peace with his butt, render the *buttcano* harmless, and blast the true ringleader, the *Great White Butt,* into outer space. *Zack Freeman* recounted his story in great detail to writer Andy Griffiths in the powerful and inspirational bestseller: *The Day My Butt Went Psycho*.

Zack Freeman
Conqueror of the Great White Butt and savior of Planet Earth. Hero of free men everywhere. See *Zack's butt*.

Zombie-buttification

Parasitic attachment of a *zombie butt* to a victim's real (or artificial) butt. Turns the victim into an eating machine that exists for the sole purpose of making the zombie butt bigger and fatter than it already is. When the host is exhausted the zombie butt will simply abandon him or her and move on in search of a new victim.

Zombie butt

A butt that is neither dead nor fully alive. Zombie butts feel no pain, have no thoughts or feelings, and possess incredible powers of regeneration, which makes them almost impossible to destroy. Driven to *zombie-buttify* potential victims, their only known weaknesses are extreme heat and a fondness for the hokeypokey.

Zombie-buttvasion

Invasion of a place — or entire planet — by *zombie butts*.

ABOUT THE AUTHOR

Andy Griffiths is the *New York Times* best-selling author of *The Day My Butt Went Psycho!*, *Zombie Butts from Uranus!*, *Butt Wars!: The Final Conflict*, *Just Stupid!*, *Just Wacky!*, *Just Annoying!*, *Just Joking!*, *Just Disgusting!*, and the Schoolin' Around series. He lives in Australia with his wife, their kids, and his butt.

WANT MORE BUTTS?